Immaculate:

Book 2 of The Gifted Series

By Ana Ban

Immaculate by Ana Ban

© 2016   Ana Ban. All rights reserved.

1.Romance 2.Fantasy 3.Paranormal

ISBN 9781520863535

First Edition

Printed in the USA

Dedicated to my sister, Denise.

Thank you for always being there for me.

You are a wonderful mother and have the most giving spirit I know.

CHAPTER 1

"If you love me only in my dreams, let me be asleep forever"

Reya, 26 years old

When I stepped into the predawn morning, I was immediately blinded. What felt like hundreds of flashes of light assaulted my eyes, and though my natural reaction was to shut them, they remained wide open. With my mouth agape, I stood frozen for a full minute.

"Can you confirm that you are pregnant?"

"Is it true that you're a virgin?"

"Do you believe this is the next coming of Christ?"

"Is this Satan's child?"

"Were you abducted by aliens?"

The allegations that were turning more ludicrous by the second were hurled at me, and when I finally forced my limbs to obey me, I ran through the crowd of reporters with my head down, but they persisted.

"Ms. Tane!" My name echoed across the dark sky like it had been shouted into a great canyon.

"A statement, Ms. Tane!"

Keys in hand, I hit the unlock button and nearly dove head first into the relative safety of the car. It was surrounded, the anxious reporters like moths to a flame, so I revved the engine to give myself some space. A few scurried back, and at the slightest opening, I hit the gas and spun into the street, narrowly missing a particularly greasy looking reporter. Free, I flew down the street and into downtown Cambridge.

The drive was silent and quick, my knuckles white on the wheel. My head spun, but I managed to think and piece together what had happened. Someone had obviously leaked the story to the press, but I wasn't so concerned with that. I was concerned, however, about the repercussions it would have on those closest to me.

There were more of the wretched creatures, unbelievably, camped out in front of the small office I spent the majority of my time at. Skipping the front door, I drove around back where only emergency drop-off vehicles were allowed. It was blocked by a lift gate and a solitary guard. He waved me through, probably having seen the crowd in the front of the building.

For once I was breaking the rules, and didn't care one bit.

I parked out of the way of any incoming emergency vehicles and hurried inside. Ben was waiting for me.

"I saw you drive past the front," he said, and ushered me into a back office.

Dropping into a chair, I studied the older man. Ben was my mentor, my confidant and my boss. We met eight years ago, when I'd applied for a filing job at his medical office. Now, I was the newest physician on his staff.

Two days ago, after three days of being sick, Ben forced me to have an exam. It bothered me at the time, because not once in my life that I could remember had I ever been sick. No colds, no allergies, not even headaches. And then, to my absolute and complete shock, to find out…

"I don't know who would have done this," Ben said, his hands twisting together. Ben was a gentle spirit, a perfect family physician. He would never seek to harm anyone, and wouldn't believe evil in others. Most of the time I was the same.

"It doesn't matter, Ben. I know it wasn't you. Whoever it was, they were probably just trying to make a buck. Don't worry about that."

"Reya, it's not right. You shouldn't be put through this."

I nodded. "Thanks, Ben. How long do you think it'll take for this to blow over?"

He shook his head. "Who knows. It's big news. I don't suppose you've seen a paper yet?" He looked to me to confirm, and when I shook my head he continued. "Front page story. They've been calling here for interviews, and Roger's been handling them." He shook his head again, but a small smile formed. "Isabel will be upset she missed all the excitement."

I smiled with him, but only briefly. Isabel's official job was receptionist, but we all knew she was the wheel that kept Hearth turning. She was also my closest friend. Currently, she was on her honeymoon and would be decidedly upset when she got back and found out the news.

I sighed with resignation. "Do you have a paper here?"

Ben nodded and rose, leading me up towards the front. A plan of action was slowly forming in my head, but it wasn't quite complete.

We walked into the front reception area, where Roger sat looking stressed but concerned. A glance at the door assured me there were still reporters, trying to nose their way inside. I gave Roger a small smile of gratitude before grabbing the paper Ben held out to me.

IMMACULATE BIRTH BY LOCAL DOCTOR

It was a half-page article. In this day and age, it was difficult to believe anyone took credence to the story. Of course, that didn't mean it wasn't true...

I scanned it quickly and noticed a picture of me, one taken when I graduated med school. Nausea crept up on me, having nothing to do with the baby. Putting the paper aside, I closed my eyes and took two deep breaths.

"Ben," I said quietly, "I have a favor to ask of you."

"Of course, Reya, anything."

Opening my eyes, I focused just on him. I could see Roger from the corner of my eye, feigning disinterest.

"Talk to the reporters. Tell them it was a mistake, give them something believable."

He nodded, and asked, "How long will you be gone?"

My look turned to surprise. "How..?"

He smiled gently. "After all this time, you're still surprised when I know you better than you know yourself. Go, Reya, take all the time you need. Your job will be here, if and when you return."

Tears sprang to my eyes, which I ruthlessly pushed down. On impulse, I hugged the man that was the only father figure I had known. "Thank you, Ben. For everything."

Stepping back, I studied him a moment longer. He looked tired, but ready to take on whatever those reporters could dish out. I turned to walk to the back, but paused by the doorway. "Tell Isabel I'll call her as soon as I'm able," I said, and continued to the door.

It was just past noon and I was sitting in the Los Angeles airport terminal, waiting for the next plane to arrive. The only thing I had brought with me was a small carry-on with a few changes of clothes. If I needed, I would buy new. My clothes wouldn't fit me much longer anyway.

The race out of Boston didn't take long. I stopped at my apartment's lease office, leaving a check to cover a few months' rent. I couldn't be sure how long I would be gone, and hoped that would cover it. There was also a lawyer I visited before I caught a flight to LA. Now, it was on to Sydney. And, from there, just another short hop to Ayers Rock.

In Ayers Rock, I hoped to learn the secret of who I was.

My parents died before I could even retain memories of them. I grew up in a state house and never gave them much thought. Everything I was, I threw into my studies to become a doctor. It was my calling, I knew that with everything inside me. And now, just six months into realizing my dream, I was magically pregnant.

Nothing in my studies prepared me for this. Dating had never been high on my list of things to do, and forget being intimate with a man.

I wasn't against it in any way. Dating, or the intimacy. Isabel was the champion dater, and I enjoyed her tales throughout the years. Her wedding had been beautiful, and I was incredibly happy for her.

There had just never been a man in my life that I felt even an iota of interest in.

Perhaps there was something wrong with me. Something different.

Of course, there *was* something different about me. I'd been diagnosed with a rare disease as a child, and had been going to a doctor weekly to receive blood transfusions. My odd disease was the first of many reasons I'd become obsessed with becoming a doctor.

Then, my abilities as a doctor went beyond the norm. It had been happening for a few years, but it wasn't something I gave much thought to. Cowardly, I thought now. It was too hard to accept, so I didn't think about it. I just used them like I would a bad feeling in the pit of my stomach.

4

Never did I think that maybe it wasn't just my ability to heal that went beyond medicine. I knew nothing of my parents. What if I was some kind of different... being? A being that could reproduce without the necessary- or at least, usual- participants?

When I'd turned 18, I had been contacted by a lawyer about an inheritance left to me. It surprised me, of course, and I signed the papers like a good girl. But since that day, I hadn't given it a second thought.

The inheritance was kept in a small bank in Ayers Rock, where the lawyer that originally handled it resided. In my hastily thrown together plan this morning, Ayers Rock became my goal.

In front of me, a TV was set to a news channel. It had been buzzing in the background, but I had been staring out the window instead. Something caught my attention and I glanced up, and let out a gasped shock at the photo that was being displayed.

"Local residents Grant and Sophia Desdemona died in a car crash yesterday afternoon, leaving their two daughters. The Desdemona's were renowned scientists and will be sorely missed. Services are being held next Saturday. Our thoughts go out to their family in their time of need."

The photo showed a happy couple, a small, dark haired woman with too-large blue eyes and a tall, blonde man with an arm wrapped around his wife. Two little girls were in the picture, little miniatures of their mother, except for one of the little girl's blonde hair.

Recognition hit swiftly, though it had been years. Possibly the strangest encounter I've had. A little girl, visiting Boston with her family, who broke her arm by a falling branch when a tree was struck by lightning. Her name was Jinx, and her mother had been a complete whack job. Or so I thought.

Jinx is a very special little girl. I know you won't understand this for years to come, but you will meet her again. And when you do, she will need your guidance. Will you promise me to do your best?

Her mother's words rang in my head. My heart leaped into my throat. Is that why this had happened? To get me to California? Was I supposed to stay here? Help this poor girl and her sister, when they had just lost their parents? Just like I had?

Australia suddenly seemed the wrong move. It didn't take long to debate. Without so much as a plan I stood, and began walking towards the exit. For the first time, I glanced towards the gate and the desk where customer service was located for the flight. For a brief second, my eyes rested upon the screen behind them, displaying the flight information.

FINAL DESTINATION: AYQ

Another image flashed in my head. Jinx's mother, just as they were leaving the hospital that day.

Do the letters AYQ mean anything to you?

They hadn't. She assured me they would. With my heart leaping to my throat once again, I walked blindly to the desk.

"Excuse me," I whispered, staring at the letters.

"Yes?" One of the cheery women answered.

"What is AYQ?"

"That's the Ayers Rock Airport. Is that where you're headed today?"

I nodded, my eyes still locked on the screen.

"Well, that plane just landed. We'll be loading shortly."

I continued to nod, and took my seat again. *You'll know what to do.*

I sure hoped so.

CHAPTER 2

The flight to Sydney was long, and I was sick twice. The helpful flight attendant put it down to motion sickness, and I didn't bother to change her mind. After the news fiasco, I didn't want any more people to know.

After landing in Sydney, I took a small charter flight to Ayers Rock. Looking back, I should have at least called the lawyer when I first found out about the inheritance, but it was pointless to regret the past.

Since I had already gone through customs in Sydney, I headed straight outside the tiny airport to snag a cab. There were two of them, with the drivers leaning against the passenger doors. The first in line grinned at me and opened the back.

"G'day, miss. American, aren't you?"

I looked at him, slightly bewildered. "That's right."

His smile widened and he gestured towards the Harvard sweatshirt I was still wearing, even though the weather in Australia was bordering on summer. "That, and you have a funny accent."

"Lucky guess," I told him, but smiled and slid into the back seat.

He climbed into the front and asked, "Where to?"

I gave him the address of the lawyer and leaned back to take in the scenery. There wasn't much around the airport but land and more land. After living in the East Coast for my entire life, the wide-open spaces were disorienting.

"First time to the Outback?"

I glanced up and met blue eyes that sparkled back at me through the rearview mirror.

"Yes. It's quite a change from what I'm used to."

"It grows on you," he commented. Something in his tone bothered me, but I couldn't put a finger on it.

"Are you from here?" I asked.

"Born and raised. You look mighty tired."

I smiled wanly and yawned. "I guess I am. Long flight."

Long, and sleepless.

He stayed quiet after that, humming quietly to himself. It was peaceful. The drive into town would take at least 20 minutes, so I settled into the seat and closed my eyes. Within seconds I was out.

I was jolted awake when the car slowed and came to a halt. Opening my eyes, I looked around what seemed to be a small encampment, in the middle of nowhere. There were no buildings, and no town, that I could see.

"Where are we?" I asked, suddenly wary.

The driver glanced back at me and met my eyes through the rearview mirror. "Sorry, miss," he said quietly.

Before I could speak, the doors on either side of me were ripped open and rough hands were grabbing my arms. I was dragged out, bag and all, and stood blinking into the bright sun. On each side of me was a man gripping my arms, and in front of me stood a man with dark skin and shrewd eyes. I felt my stomach flip.

"Reya Tane." He made it more of a statement than a question.

"Who are you?" I asked, faking more bravado than I felt.

"A man you will help, if you value your life. Bring her."

He motioned to the men holding me and they dragged me to a small tent. Shoving me inside, they set me on the floor and tied my hands and feet together with thick rope before securing me to a post in the center. My bag was flung to a side, too far for me to reach. Without a word, they left and I was alone.

Panic was a gnawing sensation, growing by the minute. Millions of scenarios raced through my mind, but two and two just refused to equal four. Where was I? Who were these men? What did they want?

Time became endless inside the small, stuffy tent. My mind wandered from the most immediate unanswered questions and went back over events that led me here. Sweat dripped down my back in long streams. I had definitely underestimated the spring season in the Northern Territory. If that's even where I still was.

The truth was, I had absolutely no clue where I was or why. While I had been sleeping in the back of the cab, we could have driven anywhere. So not only did I not know how far away Ayers Rock was, I didn't even know which direction to run if I managed to get free.

Stupid, I thought. Reckless and stupid to put my guard down. Not that I had expected to get kidnapped, but I was in a new country and should have been paying attention to my surroundings. I was just so tired.

Placing my hands over my stomach, I closed my eyes. Tired because of the baby. A thought occurred to me. Could they want me because of the baby? When I first arrived, the man knew my name. How could he possibly know my name unless they were looking for me in particular?

Letting out a sigh, I leaned against the pole I was tied to. Guess I would just have to wait and see.

When the flap finally opened, it was dark inside and out. I wasn't sure how long it had been dark, or even if a day had passed. Squinting to try to see the intruder, I almost jumped when he spoke.

"You are to come with me." Two men entered then, and untied me from the pole. They worked on the ropes at my feet also before lifting me to them. Leaving my hands tied in front, they guided me outside.

Torches stuck into the ground lit our way as we walked between two rows of tents. My eyes darted around, but there wasn't much else to see past the tents except complete darkness. They had, more than likely, planned it that way.

Near the middle of the row, they halted our progress and the lead man announced our arrival. After an order from inside, the flap was lifted and I was shoved inside.

It was well lit and surprisingly spacious, for a tent. Hesitating, I looked around while I could. There was a table before me and a cot to the left. Lanterns provided the light and a small machine produced cool air. I was grateful for the momentary relief from the heat.

The man that had originally greeted me was standing behind the desk, watching my assessment of the room. When my eyes shifted back to him, he motioned towards the chair in front of the table.

"Please, sit."

I did and watched him steadily. My voice came out harder than I expected. "What do you want with me?"

He smiled, slow and sardonic. "You have spirit. Good." He sat then and leaned back in his chair. "You have seen the reports about you?"

My heart sank and my hands wrapped around my stomach protectively. "What are you talking about?"

His eyes flicked to my hands and back again. "You know perfectly well. Though, I don't believe you've seen the latest."

Standing, he picked up scattered papers and set them before me.

The first headline popped out at me.

VIRGIN DOCTOR A MIRACLE WORKER

Another, from a different paper.

POWERFUL HEALINGS, IMMACULATE BIRTH; IS THIS THE NEXT COMING OF CHRIST?

The articles went on with eyewitness accounts of amazing recoveries, all credited to me. I remembered the names written down, the individual stories that went with them. I felt my heart actually ache in my chest.

"What is this?"

"Dear Reya, don't be shy. We've actually known about you for some time. Plans were in motion to retrieve you. Fortunately for us, you did most of the work. And, as a bonus, we'll also have your child."

Fire sparked in my eyes as I switched my glare from the papers to him. "You won't touch my child."

"Oh, but we will. Believe me, we will. So, you see, we need to keep you healthy until it is born. After that- well, your behavior over the next few months will dictate what we do with you."

"I'll never help you."

He seemed to consider my words carefully. "I believe you will. If not for me, then for your baby's sake."

My face paled, but I could still feel the burning behind my eyes. It was a silent promise to myself that no one, and nothing, would harm me or mine.

"Who are you?"

"Please forgive me, how rude. My name is Donovan Barbury."

"What do you want from me?" Deciding to play the part of the acquiescent hostage, I lowered my eyes to the floor.

"Do you know what we do here, Reya?" Staying silent, I shook my head. "We collect information. Sometimes, those we collect information from are..." he paused, and I saw his hand moving as if he were looking for the proper word, "uncooperative. Naturally, we have to ensure their cooperation, but it sometimes leads to unfortunate events, which render our informants useless. What I would like from you is to lessen the amount of time spent between sessions."

My voice was an ugly whisper of sound. "You want me to heal those you torture, so you can torture them again."

He let out a chuckle of amusement, but I still refused to look up. "Why, you are a bright one."

"I won't help you," I said through my teeth.

"I beg to differ. But we shall see. Please, come with me."

His voice and manner were perfectly gentlemanly, which only grated on my nerves. The flap of the tent opened, and immediately I felt my two guards position themselves beside me. Each securing an arm, they led me towards the end of the row of tents.

Donovan stepped to the flap first, holding it open courteously for me to enter. When I did, I gasped in shocked horror.

Blood was everywhere. And I mean, *everywhere*. The stench was enough to send me to my knees, retching from the reek, and there I would have stayed were it not for my guards lifting me to my feet. A man lay on the ground, his arms and legs tied with the customary rope, a low moan protruding through his mangled throat. He was completely motionless, and by the cuts and amount of blood surrounding him, I would have thought him dead except for that sound. Bile rose in my throat as I fought nausea, and only the fact that I had not eaten in what could possibly be days kept me from adding to the mess.

11

"I need my hands," I managed to say. I was unable to tear my eyes away from the mess of what was a man before me, so I simply waited until one of my guards untied the ropes. I moved without conscious thought, everything in me reaching out to the man in need.

Amid the gore I knelt, running my hands down the length of the man's body. Information flooded into me, but it wasn't so shocking anymore. Quickly I sorted through the information. There was intense internal bleeding, and one particularly deep cut had sliced into his liver. Closing my eyes, I shut out everything around me and allowed my instincts to take over.

There was more damage than I had ever attempted to heal at once. My body was weak from lack of food and water. But with absolute determination to save this man's life, I placed my hands directly over his liver and allowed the heat to build. It came from every cell inside me, a fiery heat that could heal with a touch. With each scrap that I could summon gathered into my hands, I sent it seeking into the man's injured form. Minutes went by and still I focused. Finally, his breathing eased, and I collapsed onto the ground beside him.

When my eyes managed to slide open, I was back in my own tent, with my feet tied together to the pole. My head ached and refused to lift off the ground. Shuffling feet came closer and paused beside my head. A cool metal pressed against my lips. The second I opened my mouth, I choked on the water hastily being poured into it. The cup was taken away, allowing me to breathe, before it was pressed once again.

"Better?" A hazy yet familiar voiced asked.

A groan was his only answer before I slipped back into the darkness.

CHAPTER 3

The next time I came to, there was a steady stream of light on my face. Groggy, but aware immediately of my predicament, I forced my eyes open to judge my surroundings.

I was still inside the small tent, in much the same position as before. My throat was dry and scratchy, and when my eyes adjusted to the light I realized the flap was open. With only my feet tied to the pole, I gingerly lifted my body off the ground using my hands.

"You're awake." It was that same distinctly familiar voice. When I turned, I recognized him immediately.

"Why did you bring me here?" It was difficult to speak, and he responded by kneeling beside me with a cup of water.

"I was under orders," he replied while I took feeble sips. It was hot and rancid. It tasted spectacular.

I studied him, hardly believing he could be part of some secret organization that was torturing people. The day I had arrived at the airport I had been exhausted, but felt comfortable with him in the cab. Either my danger radar was severely off, or this man did not belong with these heathens.

He had wavy, sandy blonde hair and calm blue eyes, with skin tanned from the sun. He looked like he should be surfing in the ocean, not holed up in some secluded camp in the middle of the desert.

"What's your name?" I asked him.

He seemed surprised by my question but answered anyway. "Aden."

"Well, Aden, I feel as if I've been run over by a truck and swallowed a large amount of sand in the process. If your boss expects me to keep this up, I need enough food and water to keep me from keeling over."

It was the best I could do under the circumstances. Silently, I was kicking myself for doing the one thing I insisted I wouldn't- help Donovan. It just wasn't in me to leave someone in pain, especially not when I could help. I figured demands were the next best thing to make up for it.

He nodded, and I saw a small smile playing at the sides of his mouth. "I'll tell him."

Standing, he took the single step it took to reach the entrance. He hesitated and looked back at me before leaving. "Reya- I *am* sorry. I know you don't understand what we do here, but it is important." With that, he left.

As soon as he disappeared I slumped back to the floor. My little speech had taken just about as much energy as I could muster, and I had a feeling I would be needing more soon.

I slept lightly until Aden returned with a tray of food and a full jug of water. Starving as I was, I ate slowly so my body wouldn't go into shock. More than likely, most of the meal would be thrown up anyway, but I had to get what nutrition I could. For a moment, I rested my hand protectively over my stomach, a gesture that was quickly becoming a habit. The little life inside of me barely seemed real. Besides the fact that there were no possible fathers, my stomach was still flat and smooth. Ben had estimated me to be only eight weeks along, so it wouldn't be too much longer before I did start to show.

"You're pregnant," Aden commented, bringing my thoughts back to the present.

I nodded and scooped up more of what I assumed to be potatoes.

"Is it true? I mean, about the," he stopped abruptly, and I was amused to see a flush of color steal into his cheeks. No, he definitely did not belong here.

"Sometimes, things happen in life that we can't explain. I have an extraordinary ability to heal people. Where did that come from? I don't know, but it *is* a gift, and one I intend to treasure. I feel the same about this child."

Aden shook his head and focused on a spot behind me. "There are so many things I've seen with my own eyes that I would have never believed had they simply been repeated to me. Sometimes, I don't believe half of it anyway."

His thoughts seemed to take him away from the moment, and I let the silence close over us for a few beats. Finally, I asked him, "Why are you here?"

He focused back on me. "We gather information."

The answer was so automatic I figured it had been drilled into his head.

It was my turn to shake my head. "No, why are *you* here?"

For a long while he was silent, and I wasn't sure if he hadn't understood my question or was just ignoring it.

"There are people," he paused with a sneer that warped his otherwise gentle features, "if you can call them people, that are truly evil in this world. I'm here to stop them."

Before I could whet my curiosity, the flap opened and Aden stood. One of my many guards entered to untie my feet before leading me down the long row of tents.

With my strength somewhat returned, I was able to heal two more people before weakness overcame me. Aden helped me back to the tent, where I immediately lay down on the floor. Refusing to pass out, I closed my eyes and took deep breaths. Once my feet were securely tied to the pole, Aden sat beside me.

"Is that really necessary?" I asked, keeping my eyes closed.

"Unfortunately, yes. Although I don't believe you could fight your way out of a paper bag right now."

I attempted a laugh but it came out strangled. "Some miracle worker I am."

"You should rest now," I heard him say, but unconsciousness was already claiming me.

Waking up in this fog-covered reality was getting just a bit old. I couldn't remember the last time my head felt clear, my body refreshed. With a groan, I opened my eyes and sat up.

"Water?" Aden asked me, holding out a canteen.

Gratefully, I took a swallow. My stomach rolled but it stayed down. "How long was I out?"

"Just an hour or so. I'm to bring you to the dunny."

Raising an eyebrow, I asked skeptically, "The dunny?"

He grinned in response. "The little girl's room."

"Oh." Gingerly I stood, waiting for him to untie my feet. Following him outside, I decided to make more conversation. "So, you're my babysitter, huh?"

"Someone has to be," he answered.

Behind the back of the tent was a port-a-potty. Very elegant.

Quickly, I did my business and came back out. It would be my mission to spend as little time in there as possible.

"Where to now?" I asked.

He led me around to the front of the tent once again. "Home sweet home," he muttered.

When I entered, I was surprised to see another tray of food on the floor. "Wow, room service. I didn't realize this was a full-service establishment."

Aden chuckled and knelt to the ropes. "Only the best for our guests here, miss."

With the tray in hand, I sat and watched Aden. If I was ever going to get out of here, I had to have an ally. He seemed to be my best bet.

First, I needed more information.

"Why were you picked to baby-sit?"

He glanced up for a second and back down at his work. "It was more of a volunteer."

"I can't be that interesting, passed out most of the time."

Finished, he had no choice but to look back at me. "Some of the men here can be brutes. Which is fine, with the kind of work done. But you, you've done nothing wrong. And I can't let them treat you the same as they would another captive."

"Thank you," I murmured. He shrugged. After a pause, I asked quietly, "What happened to you?"

He glanced away, and I waited patiently for his answer. I refused to let him evade me again. "I had a sister. She was young, beautiful, full of life. When I was 18, our parents died; she was just 10 years old. I raised her. She loved going on adventures. If there was a piece of jungle unrecorded, she wanted to see it. If there was an unexplored cave, she wanted to be in it." Just then his eyes turned ice cold, a big contrast from the clear blue of the sea. "Two years ago, she turned 20, and was set on this particular forest area of New Zealand. Even though I had a bad feeling about it, I couldn't say no to her. So, we went."

He went quiet again, and I could tell even after two years his memories were fresh. Reaching out to him, I placed a hand on his arm. Surprised, he glanced down at it as if he had forgotten I was there.

"You don't have to tell me, it's all right," I soothed.

He shook his head adamantly. "I want you to know. This is why I'm here." Letting out a deep breath, he continued. "On our second day hiking, these shadows crossed over us. I realize it sounds crazy, but they were giant and when I looked around, there was nothing above us but trees. Not even wind. I called out to Aurelia and she turned, but before she could reach me, all these men surrounded us. I mean, out of nowhere. I fought my way to her side, but one of the men slammed his hands against my chest."

Absently, he rubbed a hand across his heart. "It dropped me, just like that. I'm pretty sure I had a heart attack, though I never saw a doctor to have it confirmed. All I could do was lay there on the ground, watching. Three of them stood around Aurelia, making these motions with their hands. She stood so still, and I knew something was wrong because she's such a fighter. And then they," he paused, staring at me, "vanished."

Goosebumps had started with his story and as it finished, a shiver ran down my spine. Lightly I rubbed my arms, willing the feeling away. "I'm so sorry, Aden. That must have been awful for you."

He nodded, and continued. "I'm not sure how long I was out in that forest, all alone. Eventually, I saw a face. Donovan. He found me, brought me here and I've been working towards finding these fiends and bringing them to justice ever since."

Seeing the utter determination in his eyes, I waited a few beats before speaking. "You know, Aden, up until a couple years ago, I didn't know I was able to help people the way I do. And, up until a couple days ago, I didn't know there might be others like me. Am I so bad?"

He looked up sharply with denial on his tongue. "Of course not."

"Well, in my experience, there are good people and there are bad people. Just because a group of terrorists comes from a certain country doesn't mean the entire country is bad. Just because a father is horrid doesn't mean the son will be. And just because this group of men took your sister, doesn't mean that everyone with their abilities wouldn't have given their life to defend her."

There was a small hesitation, and I knew this was something that had gone through his mind before. "They still need to be stopped."

"I absolutely agree. But how do you know the people that are in those tents have even done anything wrong?"

He was silent, and I didn't dare press him further. Aden had been hurt, and wanted to stop others from going through the same. I couldn't fault him for that. But somewhere, no matter how buried it might be through Donovan's lies, there was the knowledge of right and wrong.

"You'll want to be finishing that meal," he finally said quietly. "They'll be wanting you to go out again tonight."

I nodded and dutifully ate a spoonful. It looked like mush and tasted like dirt, but I ate every last drop.

"There's something else I'm going to need if I'll be staying here any amount of time," I spoke again after clearing my plate.

"What's that?" he asked, seeming genuinely curious.

"This probably won't help convince you that I'm normal," I smiled at him, "but I have a rare blood disease in which my red blood cells are unable to reproduce. I've been getting blood transfusions once a week as long as I can remember."

Aden was staring at me, so much that I began to feel self-conscious. He seemed to shake himself out of it, though, and spoke. "I'll let Donovan know," he promised. "What blood type do you need?"

"Actually, any. I'm AB-positive, so I'm able to take in any type."

He seemed to ponder this more before crouching to the ties on my feet.

"I'll make sure you get what you need."

When he led me out again, there was no other guard to walk with me. Perhaps I had played the good hostage convincingly enough to lower my security. It was a good start.

"How many people are being held here?" I whispered as we walked along.

"Six, besides you."

Aden led me inside the last in the row of tents, and my heart sank. There was only one smell that could so easily roll my stomach over. Death.

I approached the figure slowly, holding a hand out for Aden to stay back. Kneeling beside the slumped man, I expected the worst as I ran my hands along his exposed chest. As I passed over his heart, I felt hope blossom when I sensed a pulse. It was sluggish and much too far apart, but it was there.

With new urgency, I placed my hands directly over the heart and felt the warmth rush out of me. There were unfamiliar drugs in his system, something that I filed away for future reference. The drugs were effective and deadly.

Once they were pushed through his system and his heart rate was once again steady, I sank back on my heels and closed my eyes. "What kind of drugs are they using?"

"I'm not sure. They are mostly experimental, created by people who work for Donovan."

I shook my head sadly. More than likely, none of these men had done anything wrong. It was just such a waste, and all I was doing was prolonging the suffering.

"Reya, I..."

With effort, I opened my eyes and glanced over at Aden.

"There's someone here. Someone that I want you to look at. Donovan didn't actually say to have you look at him, but there's something about him, and..."

I nodded. "I understand. How bad is he?"

He shrugged. "I really can't tell. What he's been through, no one should ever survive. I don't know how he's done it. And he hasn't said a word, not one since he arrived. His body is so weak, and yet when he looks at you, it's like looking at raw power. I'm sorry, I know that sounds strange."

I managed a weak laugh. "Everything sounds strange nowadays. Let me have a look."

He nodded and led me out. Across the way was a tent set off from the others with two guards in front of the entrance. We slipped inside and I froze at the door.

Unlike the others, this man was secured in a pillory, with his head and hands sticking through the small gaps in the wood. On top of that, metal manacles secured his wrists and feet instead of the rope I was getting used to. Every piece of exposed skin showed crisscrossed marks of torture. His head was slumped, his long dark hair hanging nearly to the ground.

Though I was frozen in a mix of terror and disgust, my feet began stepping one in front of the other until I stood before him. Oblivious to the room and Aden behind me, I stared down at the top of his head.

He looked dead. His entire body was limp, motionless. Unexpectedly, tears brimmed in my eyes but still I stood, frozen to the spot.

Without so much as a warning, his hand snaked out and gripped my arm. One subtle flick of his wrist and I was on my knees before him, my arm on fire with pain. But I didn't register the pain. Slowly, his head lifted and his dark eyes met mine.

I was falling. Straight through a whirlwind of darkness, down a seemingly endless pit. Swirls of images, pieces of memory slapped at me and just as quickly were gone again. My head spun as hundreds of scenes played out within a split second. Greens, reds, browns. Faster they flew at me. Leaves, water, flowers. A soft song, a light breeze. Knife wounds. A big, soft bed in the middle of a forest.

My breath sucked in; a gasp of surprise, shock and bewilderment. Carefully, I pulled myself away from the images and focused wholly on the man before me, his eyes, a glittering obsidian, focused solely back on me. A man I had never seen before in my life.

Yet, without a doubt, I knew I was looking into the eyes of my child's father.

CHAPTER 4

Reya, 18 years old

A lawyer's office was the last place I wanted to be on my eighteenth birthday. Well, I suppose the last place would be a torture chamber somewhere in the Middle East, but I digress.

The stuffy office held an abundance of fake plants and plaques on the walls. Behind the ornate wood desk sat a well-dressed man with hollow eyes. With my hands folded tightly in my lap, I listened to his droning and waited patiently for when I could leave. I had dressed appropriately for the day in a black pantsuit with a white collared shirt, my unruly hair pulled into a bun. As it was, I was itching to get back into jeans and a tee. If this lawyer didn't hurry, my feet may just get up and leave of their own accord.

It was already late afternoon, but the day was far from over. I'd be heading straight back to school to take the last midterm before Winter Break.

"So, you're the youngest person at Harvard right now, isn't that right?"

Switching my focus back to the man in front of me, I forced a smile and nodded politely. "That's correct."

"What are you studying?" He asked.

"I plan on finishing Med School," I replied.

"That's great. We can always use good doctors. Well, just sign here and the funds will be yours."

Quickly I scrawled my signature and stood.

"So what do you plan to do with the inheritance?" He asked, following my action.

"Invest," I answered without embellishment. The truth was, I had been saving my entire life. Between that and scholarships, my schooling was paid for and I didn't plan on touching the money. The only reason I agreed to the meeting was because I knew if I didn't, the lawyer would have harassed me until I gave in.

I took his proffered hand and left the office. As soon as my feet hit the pavement, I yanked the band from my hair to allow it to fall freely. It was thick and dark with red streaks in the right light. When free, it swung towards my lower back. Reaching my car parked a block away, I exchanged the suit jacket for a large and comfortable sweatshirt. The pants would have to suffice until after the exam.

The air was crisp with winter, though the first snow had already come and gone. Hurrying through the courtyard, I noted the other students whose only thoughts were the freedoms of the month vacation. I could almost feel the excitement pounding at me, expecting me to join in. There was no reason to. I'd be working, a filing job for a medical office that I was lucky to secure so early on in my studies. Most would be going home to celebrate the holidays. I had no home.

My parents had died too early for me to even have memories of them. Throughout the years, I was a ward of the state, excelling in my studies not because I was necessarily smart, but because I tried harder than others. It was a surprise when, six months earlier, a lawyer had tracked me down to let me know my parents had left me an inheritance, and I would receive it on my eighteenth birthday. It was all I had of them, a chunk of money sitting in some offshore account. There it would stay, until I came up with a better idea.

After three hours, classes were officially done. I found myself with two days and no pressing matters. Perhaps it should have been a nice break. After all, I was young and independent. There should be a million things to do on a night such as this.

I stopped at a bookstore on the way home. To my credit, I picked up a fictional story. It had been years since I had read something other than the required. And since I was feeling extra spunky, I also picked up a carton of Ben and Jerry's and some bubble bath. No one ever accused me of not knowing how to have a good time.

Filtered sunlight found its way through the canopy of trees to touch my face. It was warm, as it always was here. This expanse of forest had been my escape since childhood. In my darkest and loneliest hours, I conjured this place in my dreams. Lush grass allowed me to walk barefoot, and a simple white sundress swished around my knees. Following the well-known path towards the stream, I felt happy and at peace.

Birds sang a light song in the quiet and I found myself humming along. Though my body seemed insubstantial, I could feel the ground beneath my feet and the moist air surrounding me. It smelled sweet, like freshly bloomed flowers.

The steady flow of water was calming and tranquil. I began to walk downstream, following the lithe, colorful bodies that swam lazily through the currents. Occasionally my foot would dip into the water, sending a shock wave out. Although surprisingly warm, the water felt refreshing against my skin. Wading out calf deep, I stood and gazed at my surroundings. Greens of every shade made up the majority of vegetation, with brightly colored flowers littering the forest floor. Everything was always in full bloom here, no matter the time of year I drew it into my subconscious.

Continuing in the shallow water, I rounded a bend and paused. Before me was an intruder to my forest, crouched low beside the shore. His gaze was intent on the stream, as if he, too, was using it to soothe.

Staying perfectly still, I studied the stranger. His hair was dark as night and flowed to his shoulders, his skin a shade darker than my own. While his body seemed fit, his face, when he lifted it to mine, looked ravaged. We stood staring at one another; strangers yet familiar in this make-believe land.

"Who are you?" I asked, still not moving.

"You know me," he answered.

Shaking my head in denial, I took a few steps towards him. "This is my place. I have never seen you here before."

For a moment confusion flitted across his perfectly chiseled face, but it quickly vanished. "What are you doing here?"

"I come here to escape. What are you doing here?"

A brief smile found his lips, not quite reaching his dark, fathomless eyes. "The same."

"Reya Tane?"

At the sound of my name, I glanced up at the receptionist. "Yes?"

"They're ready for you. Go on back."

It was the first day at my internship for Hearth Medical. Mostly I would do paperwork, and learn the ins and outs of the file room. There wasn't much else I *could* do at this point.

In the small room that passed for an office, a man with graying hair and a kind smile stood to shake my hand. "Reya, nice to see you again. Please, sit."

"Thank you, Dr. Brooke."

"Oh, dear, call me Ben, please."

With a smile of acknowledgement, I sat and listened to his instructions. Today I would be trained on the computer and phones, after getting a thorough tour of the center. It was relatively small, with regular operating hours. There was a small skeleton crew for the night shift to watch over any patients that needed to stay overnight. Otherwise, it was mainly average check-ups and a few broken bones.

When we were through with the tour, I sat down with the woman at the reception desk named Isabel. She had lots of curly brown hair, green eyes that seemed to miss nothing, and a smile for everyone. My best guess at her age was early twenties.

"Hi, I'm Isabel, but most people just call me Isy. Reya? That's such a pretty name. I'll be training you today, but mostly you won't be up here, unless it's to help out with breaks. Ben likes everyone to know at least the basics of each section, so we can cover each other. Oh, I love your bracelet," she touched it lightly with two fingers.

I wasn't sure if Isy had taken a breath during that entire speech. "Thank you," I told her.

"Okay, let's start with the phone system. It's pretty basic, 'Hello, thank you for calling Hearth Medical, how may I help you?' This is the hold button, obviously, it says hold. So, I hear you're at Harvard, that must be exciting. Lots of hunks down on campus, huh?" She added the last with a wink. "Here's the list of each section's phone extension, so you can transfer."

I could see conversation with Isy wouldn't require much on my part, and that suited me fine.

At home that night, I spent some time with my plants on the small patio attached to the apartment. The complex was a long row of one and two bedrooms, each with a private patio in the back. Though I had never had a yard for a garden, I had always kept flowering plants in my room. I was lucky, with the orphanage that had taken me in as a child. Each of us had our own small rooms and good schooling.

Now, with so much work to do with college, it was precious personal time that I truly believed kept my sanity.

With winter setting in, most of the plants were dormant. I had a pot of witch-hazel, which bloomed during the winter, and cut some of the flowers to bring inside.

The next few weeks went by quickly, and a few days before the end of winter break, Ben called me back into his office.

"Reya, you've been a huge help around here, and I was wondering if you'd like to stay on during regular semester," he said.

"That would be great," I said with a grin.

"Good. Talk to James about your schedule, and he'll work you in. We'll stick to 20 hours or less, and let me know if it gets too much. I know how tough med school can get."

"That shouldn't be a problem. Thank you," I added with sincerity.

He nodded his dismissal, and I walked out with a small bounce to my step.

CHAPTER 5

The stream was clear and calm as I walked along beside It, humming a nonsense tune. The voice should have startled me, but this was a dream.

"You look happy."

Turning, I saw the man standing behind me. He hadn't been there a moment ago, but that didn't seem strange. Our last meeting had been cut short, and I hadn't even asked his name.

"I am happy. Today I got asked to stay on at a clinic full time."

He took a step closer, and there was only a few feet separating us. "You're a doctor?"

With a small sway to make my baby blue dress twirl around my knees, I grinned. "Not yet. But I will be."

"What is your name?"

"Reya. What's yours?"

"Tristan."

"Nice to meet you, Tristan. Even though you are intruding."

"Intruding? But I live here."

"How could you live here? I made this place up."

I watched as his smile cleared the lines on his face. "Then you must have made me up as well."

Slowly, I made a show of inspecting him. With a shrug, I conceded, "I suppose I could have done worse."

He laughed, and the deep timber was in perfect harmony to the light tinkling of the stream. We began walking together as if it were the most natural thing in the world.

"I wonder what kind of trees these are," I gestured towards a group not far from the stream.

"Guava," Tristan answered, and, stopping, pulled a fruit down. He offered it to me, which I took without hesitation. Biting into the soft flesh, I murmured in pleasure.

"Mm. This is good."

"You've never had it?" He asked, surprised.

"No. Not the actual fruit, anyway. I've had the juice, but it's not quite the same."

"You should come here more often. Perhaps there is more I can share with you."

A brow rose as I turned to him. "Maybe I will."

Isabel greeted me with her signature smile when I walked in on my first official day as a full-time employee. "Hey, honey, I got Roger to cover the desk for lunch, so we can take it together. I had the craziest dream last night and I want to know what you think."

Over the last month, I had found out a lot about Isabel and genuinely enjoyed her company. One thing about her was, conversations were never boring.

"Sure thing. I'm on file duty today, but I'll be up at 11:30."

We walked down the street to a deli at lunch, completely bundled in parkas, gloves, hats and scarves. Winter had fully set in, and it was not happy this year.

"Man-oh-man it's cold out there. We must be nuts living here." Isabel stomped out her boots and unwrapped herself when we found a table.

"I know. Isn't it great?" I grinned at her.

She rolled her eyes at me and plopped down. "I forget who I'm talking to, Ms. I-Never-Get-Cold. Oh, that turkey and cranberry looks good."

"You get that every time," I pointed out.

She shrugged. "It looks good every time. Okay, so I had this dream last night. Remember I was telling you about Kevin?" Kevin was the latest in a string of romances Isabel graced me with each week. "Well, in this dream, I'm at my parent's house having dinner, and Kevin walks in. He says, 'Hi, Mom,' and kisses my mom on the cheek. And then, after dinner, we all sit down in the living room and start playing instruments and singing. What do you think that means?"

"Maybe you're actually related to Kevin and your subconscious is telling you to stay away."

"Oh, whatever. I think it means that he's going to propose. Or maybe I should become a rock star." She looked off and thought about it. "Nah. Too much work."

I laughed, shaking my head. "I don't think dreams really mean anything. It's just our memories playing out in strange ways."

"Oh, come on. What's the last dream you had?"

"I don't dream," I told her.

"What do you mean? Everybody dreams."

"Okay then, I don't remember my dreams. I never have."

Isy's eyes bugged out. "Really? Like, never? No nightmares as a kid, no hot sex dreams now?"

Wrong time to take a sip of tea. I choked, attempting to laugh and swallow simultaneously. When my throat cleared, I managed to say, "No, definitely none of those."

"Too bad. I always enjoy a good love scene."

There was a light drizzle falling through the trees, just enough to get wet but not uncomfortable. I lay down in the grass and closed my eyes, enjoying the mist soaking into my skin. It smelled wonderful, the rain bringing out the scents of the vegetation surrounding me.

"You're getting all wet," Tristan's voice was close.

I smiled and kept my eyes closed. "I know."

"Strange girl," I heard him mutter, and sensed him lying down next to me.

"Nice, isn't it?" I asked him

"I suppose it could grow on you."

Opening my eyes, I turned my head to look at him. He was inches away from me, staring back.

"Where have you been?" He lifted his hand to sweep away a stray strand of hair from my face.

"Working, I guess. I work hard."

"You should take a vacation," he said.

With a smile, I closed my eyes again, turning my face up to the drops. "Didn't you know? This is my vacation."

"You said you would come here more often."

Keeping my eyes closed, a small smile played at my lips. "I said maybe."

"I've missed you."

"How could you miss me? You barely know me."

"I know you."

It was said so quietly, so sincerely, it made me turn my head to look at him again. "How?"

"I don't know. Don't you feel it too?"

I shrugged. "This is just a dream. It doesn't mean anything."

"You don't believe that." As he spoke, his hand slid under mine. His other reached across to enclose it. The heat was almost unbearable. "You feel that," he continued quietly. "Your heart reacts to my touch."

"And yours? Does it react to my touch?"

His eyes, that had been staring down at our joined hands, met mine again. "Everything inside me reacts to you."

Over the summer, I went to full time at Hearth, and began to sit in on more patient exams. In the middle of July, a little girl came in with a fractured arm and a cracked rib.

"Hi there," I said, coming into the room. On the bed sat a small girl with smoky blue eyes too large for her face and pitch black hair in complete disarray. She gave me a shy smile as I sat on the stool next to her. I glanced over at her mother, and it was like looking at a larger replica of the little girl. The mother's eyes grew even larger, but didn't say anything.

Shrugging off the reaction, I turned to the little girl. It wasn't the first time a patient had thought me too young for this work.

"What's your name, sweetie?"

"I'm Jinx," she said softly.

"How old are you, Jinx?"

She sat up straighter. "Six and three quarters."

I suppressed a smile. "So, can you tell me what happened before Dr. Ben comes in? That way he can help you a bit quicker."

When she spoke, her voice was clear and surprisingly articulate.

"We were at the Longfellow house on the tour, and Desi and I were playing in the grass outside. There were clouds, but it wasn't raining yet, so we were running around before we had to drive again. Then lightning struck this big tree, but Desi didn't see it, so I pushed her out of the way and a branch fell on me." When she finished, she looked down as if she was ashamed.

"Oh, my, you must be so brave. Is Desi your sister?"

She nodded, still looking down.

"Is she okay?"

"Yeah. She got a couple scratches when she fell, and then she came back and helped me. She's real strong."

"It sounds like it. So where does it hurt?" She showed me her arm and the side that hurt.

"So, are you guys just visiting here?" I asked as I stood.

"Yes. We live all the way in California."

"Wow. That's pretty far. I'm going to go talk to Dr. Ben for a minute and he'll be right in, okay?"

She nodded and smiled at me. "Thank you."

I found Ben in the hall and gave him a quick run-down before giving Isabel a break. A few minutes after I sat down, Jinx's mother came up to the desk.

"Reya?" She asked.

Surprise flitted across my face before realizing I was wearing a name tag. "Yes, how can I help you?"

"I wanted to thank you. You worked well with Jinx."

I was surprised at the compliment. By the look that she had given me in the office, I thought she was disapproving.

She hesitated a moment, glancing over her shoulder before continuing. "I only have a minute; my husband and daughters are signing paperwork. This will sound crazy, but I have to tell you something."

"Okay," I said, not sure what I was agreeing to.

"Jinx is a very special little girl. I know you won't understand this for years to come, but you will meet her again. And when you do, she will need your guidance. Will you promise me to do your best?"

I was absolutely bewildered. Was everyone in California this nutty?

She grabbed my hand and looked me in the eyes. Even though my body temperature was higher than normal, her skin was so hot it felt as if it were burning my hand. My natural reaction was to pull away, but she held tight.

"Are you sick? You're burning up. Let the doctor look at you," I began, but she was shaking her head.

When she answered, it was if she hadn't even heard my concern. "Please. I realize how crazy this sounds, and I assure you I'm not insane. I only want what's best for my girls. Promise me?"

Without actually intending to, I found myself nodding. The tension visibly drained from her face. "Thank you," she whispered.

Behind her, Jinx and what I presumed to be her sister and father walked up. Jinx's sister was a spitting image of Jinx, except with blonde hair, like her father, and instead of smoky blue eyes, hers were bright.

With a huge smile, Jinx showed me her cast. "Will you sign it? I've never had a cast before, and you're supposed to have people sign them," she told me.

"Of course," I told her, still a bit shaken. I'm not sure if anyone could deny this little girl anything. I glanced at her sister, who stood protectively by her. Both girls and their mom were strikingly beautiful.

They turned to leave, but their mom stayed behind. "One more thing," she said, leaning over the desk. "Do the letters AYQ mean anything to you?"

I could only shake my head.

"They will. I'm not sure when, but you'll know what to do. Thank you again."

And with that, she turned and walked away. I stared after her, dumbfounded.

CHAPTER 6

"You are too thin."

My eyes narrowed as I glanced at Tristan. "Excuse me? I thought this was my subconscious, not my conscious."

He chuckled but shook his head. "Perhaps I am both. You need to eat more. Soon you will float away on a light wind."

On a huff, I turned and strode away. Of course I didn't eat right. I never ate right. Who had time for that nonsense? But I came here to escape, not to be harassed!

There was a tug on my arm that halted my progress. The touch was warm and sent that same jolt of pleasure through me as the first time. "Please, tau o te ate, *don't go."*

With a brow raised, I asked, "Tau o te ate? What's that mean?"

"It means several things in my language. It is a term of endearment. Does it bother you that I call you that?" He stood perfectly still waiting for my answer, as if he were holding his breath.

"I suppose not. It's pretty. Just don't get any ideas." I turned and began walking again, along the edge of the stream. Slower this time, though, so Tristan could walk beside me.

"What ideas should I not be having?" He asked innocently.

"Oh, please. You know exactly what ideas I mean."

"I'm afraid I do not. You will have to educate me on this."

Sighing, I gave him a sidelong glance. "Well, it's not like you're real anyway. I suppose it wouldn't matter what ideas you got."

"That is true, tau o te ate, *any ideas I have will actually be from you. So, they must be good ideas, to have come from you."*

Playfully, I slapped his arm. "Such a sweet talker. Didn't know that was in my subconscious."

"Perhaps we should find out what else is in there," he commented, and I interpreted his tone a second too late.

He wrapped two strong arms around my waist, and to my horror I let out a squeal as, with one running leap, he cannon-balled us both into the river.

Fall came quickly, and with it a full schedule. After struggling a few weeks to keep up with school and work, I was forced to drop back the days at Hearth to two. Ben understood, of course, having been through it himself, but I hated leaving him short.

"You work too hard," he told me one day in October.

I smiled up at him from the desk I was at. "I enjoy what I do."

He frowned, and sat down beside me. "There is more to life than work. When's the last time you went out, had fun? Do you even have friends?"

"Sure. Isabel is my friend. And we had lunch on Tuesday."

He shook his head and smiled. "That's because she dragged you out of here kicking and screaming. And you only took 20 minutes. Look," he rested a hand on my arm, "if you listen to any advice I give you, let it be this. Do not be consumed with this. Life is meant to be lived. Enjoy it."

Silently I nodded and watched him leave the room. I did enjoy life. Didn't I?

At closing time, I walked toward the reception area and was stopped by Isy.

"Hey hon, what are you up to?"

With a shrug, I answered, "Just heading home."

"Well," she said, her eyes lighting up. "I just found out about this place down on Main, and its ladies' night tonight. What do you say? We'll dance the night away," she emphasized this with some over-enthusiastic chair dancing.

I sighed. "Did Ben put you up to this?"

"What? No! I try to get you to go out all the time." Her mouth turned into a pout as my eyes squinted into a glare. "Okay, okay, he may have mentioned something about showing you how to enjoy life, but I've been wanting to take you here anyway. What do you say?"

With a defeated groan, I followed Isy out the door. "Fine. But I can leave anytime I want."

She grinned at me. "Sure thing. Now, what do you have to wear?"

Two hours later, I was staring at a reflection in the mirror that couldn't possibly be me. My hair was curled in long ringlets and left down. Isy had outfitted me in a... *dress...* that was black, off the shoulder, and well above my knees. Black boots that went up my calf were strapped on my feet and globs of make-up painted my face. I was horrified.

"What in the world did you do to me?" I asked Isy, with a hitch in my voice that was just a little too close to panic.

She let out a gut-wrenching laugh before answering. "Oh, honey, you look perfect. No one will even card you. Don't worry; it's one of those 18 and over just in case they do. All right, let's roll."

I wrapped myself in a black coat longer than the dress and followed Isabel out. We had opted for walking, since the club was only a few blocks from my apartment. More than likely, Isabel would be crashing on my couch tonight.

There was a line at the club a few people long when we arrived. Since it was ladies' night, we were let in immediately. I was grateful for that, since the weather had already turned and the nights were freezing. We dropped our coats at the door and went to the bar. Isabel was right- they didn't card me. She ordered some kind of concoction that she assured me would taste good and led me to a row of tables in the back.

The music was pounding, and the dance floor was packed. Lights were set to dim and I found myself squinting to see through the murk.

"What is this?" I asked after tasting the brown liquid in my glass.

"Kahlua and Cream. You like coffee, so I figured that would work for you." She sipped her own drink and grinned. "They sure didn't skip on the Kahlua."

As far as alcohol went, my experiences were limited. Actually, make that non-existent. But she was right, again. It *was* good.

Two guys approached us and asked us to dance. Isabel agreed immediately and grabbed my arm before I could object. She stayed close by, but picked one of the guys to dance with and shoved me in front of the other.

I gave him a tentative smile but didn't move. "You look nervous," he yelled into my ear. "My name's Carl. What's yours?"

"Reya," I yelled back near his ear. Luckily, with the boots on, I didn't have to stand on tippy-toe to do so.

"Just go with the flow," he told me, and grabbed my hips.

I did my best to follow along, and eventually got into the pattern. This lasted for two songs before I managed to catch Isabel with my death look. She grinned and said something into her partner's ear, then grabbed my hand again and led me back to the table.

"You all right?" She asked when we were alone.

"Yeah. Sorry, I just never…"

Her eyes widened and she leaned closer. "You've never…?"

I shrugged. "Danced and- whatever. This is all new to me."

She nodded, but her eyes gleamed with excitement. "This is going to be fun. I get to teach you all kinds of stuff."

I watched as she clapped her hands together like a giddy little schoolgirl. Suddenly I had an odd sensation of impending doom.

"Let's go back out, just the two of us. We'll keep the guys away for now, okay?"

I took a deep breath and a gulp of the drink before nodding. She led me to the middle of the floor and began moving her hips in ways I wasn't sure were safe. Slowly, I followed along. Isabel obviously was a natural and I probably looked like an elephant on roller skates, but after a while I found myself enjoying the freedom of being in a large crowd making a complete fool of myself. Before I knew it I was grinning and twirling like an idiot.

After an hour and another drink, I was relaxed but overheated. I grabbed Isy and fanned my face, and she understood. There was a side door that led to a small alley, where people could go to smoke without leaving the building and standing in line again. I slipped out and found a piece of wall unoccupied. The air felt refreshing now instead of cold, and I took some deep breaths to help cool my body off.

It didn't take long and I was about to go back in when a figure blocked my view. It was a man I recognized from inside- he had been dancing close to us all night.

"Hey there sugar, where you goin'?"

A shiver of fear swept down my spine at his tone, but I managed a small smile. "Back inside to dance. Would you like to join me?" I figured Isy could help me out once I was back inside.

Instead, he took a step closer to me. "Oh yeah," he said, his breath reeking of alcohol. "I'd like to join you."

He grabbed my upper arms and shoved me against the wall. My breath came out in a gasp, and pain shot through my chest. Panicked, I glanced towards the door. The alley was completely empty.

"There's nobody here, sugar. You know you want this. Why else would you come out here, all alone?" One hand crept up to my neck, his fingers wrapping around my throat. "One scream and I'll squeeze, understand?"

"Get away from me," I managed through clenched teeth.

He jerked me away and slammed me back into the wall. Tears leaked down my face from the pain, but I kept my eyes on his.

"Oh, you like that, don't you? You like a little pain? Well, I'll give you a little pain. Oh, yeah, I'll give you everything you need."

Disgust clogged my throat and I made an effort to get away. It only tightened his grip on my arm and throat. He leaned towards me until his mouth was against my ear. "Squirm all you want, sugar, I like it."

His hands released and grabbed at my breasts hard enough to leave bruises. Taking the chance, I brought both hands up to his chest. "I said, get away from me," I bit out and pushed with all my might with both hands. He didn't budge an inch.

"I knew you'd be a feisty one. Keep fighting. It'll make it better."

Attempting to think, I tried to bring one leg in between his so I could go for a knee to the groin. He was there quick, shoving between my legs with his and blocking my shot. I let out a frustrated groan and it only egged him on. His hands were everywhere, and I was desperate to get away. With everything in me, I gave a last-ditch attempt to shove him away. I felt an electric spark tingle through my fingertips and this time, it worked.

I saw him stumble back, his hands clenched to his chest. I didn't stick around to see what would happen next- I bolted.

"Help!" I cried out, shoving the door open. "HELP!" I repeated, and although I knew I was hysterical, it grabbed the attention of the two security guards closest. They made their way to me and I pointed to the door. "He- there was a man- and he- he tried to..." Nothing more came out because I burst into tears.

Isabel appeared, wrapping her arms around me. Dimly I noticed the two security guards open the door, and more commotion broke out.

"Call an ambulance!" I heard one say, and a rush of people crowded the small entryway. Isabel escorted me towards the front, away from the on-lookers.

"Honey? What happened?" She asked gently, holding me at arm's length.

I shook my head, feeling a little ridiculous. With a swipe at the tears with the back of my hand, I tried to talk. "I was just getting some air, and when I was coming back in, this guy just appeared. He pushed me against the wall, knocked the wind out of me. And then he tried to…" I couldn't get the word out. Luckily, I didn't have to.

Isabel pulled me back into her arms and rocked me gently. "It's okay, honey, it's okay."

A half hour later, I had given my statement to both the head of security and the police that showed up. A stretcher had come and taken the man away, but I still didn't know what was wrong with him.

When the call to 9-1-1 was made, they cleared out the reluctant crowd and put on the regular lights. I was sitting wrapped in a blanket at one of the tables, a bottle of water in my hand. Isabel was speaking to the security also, though she hadn't seen anything. When she came back over, she had a solemn look on her face.

"We can go now," she told me.

I nodded and stood. "Do they know what happened to him?"

Isabel put an arm around my shoulders and led me to the front door. "He," she hesitated, throwing a nervous look down at me. "Died. They say he had a heart attack."

CHAPTER 7

"Are you all right?"

I was sitting on a low, thick branch of a tree that served as a surprisingly comfortable chair. When Tristan spoke, I glanced up.

"Of course."

He stepped closer, studying my features. "Why are you lying to me?"

"What do you mean?"

"I felt your fear and your pain. Something happened to you."

I stood up and walked away from him. "How do you know that?"

"I told you. I felt it."

"That doesn't make any sense." Turning back towards him, I searched his face. His features were so familiar to me now, I felt as if I'd always known him.

"You made me up, remember? Of course, I know when something is wrong. Please tell me, tau o te ate." He stepped closer again, and brushed a hand over my hair, resting it on my cheek.

I leaned into the warmth with a sigh. "A man tried to hurt me," I began, but paused when I felt him tense. Looking up into his eyes, I continued, "He didn't. I fought him, and I'm not sure really what happened. I just remember having my hands on his chest and pushing with all my strength. He let go and later they told me he had a heart attack."

His hand had returned to his side, and he stood just watching me. I turned and walked away again, pacing back and forth.

"It doesn't feel right. He was younger, fit, not at all a profile for a heart attack. And," I paused again, looking back at Tristan, "as I ran, I noticed he was grabbing his chest. It didn't seem strange at the time, but he was grabbing it right where my hands were. Could I have caused this?"

Tristan shook his head. "Do not ask questions you do not wish to know the answers to."

When I woke, it was to the smell of eggs and bacon. After a few moments of utter confusion, I realized Isabel had stayed over.

Pulling on a robe, I wandered out to the kitchen and found Isabel at the stove, dancing to a silent tune. It made me smile, as she always did. Nothing seemed to bring her down, not even early mornings.

"That smells delicious."

She spun around and gave me a grin. "Hey, hon, hope you don't mind, I made myself at home. Thought the smell might wake you. How are you feeling?"

"Oh, I'm fine, thanks. I do have a little headache, but I figure that's from my first experience with Kahlua."

She set the food on plates and took a seat at the table. "That'll do it. You sure you're okay?"

I nodded and took a bite of eggs. "Nothing actually happened. If anything, it'll make me more aware of my surroundings. Maybe I'll take a couple defense classes or something."

"That would be fun. Let me know if you do, I'll go with you."

I smiled and dug in. "What time do you work today?"

"Not until 9:00, so I'll head straight from here. I brought extra clothes with me yesterday."

"Yeah, I know," I grinned, remembering the multitude of outfits she had me try on.

She grinned back. "Oh, hey, who's Tristan?"

The name wasn't familiar, but it brought an unexpected twist to my gut. I glanced up. "I don't know a Tristan."

"Oh. Well, I got up to use the bathroom last night and I heard you mutter his name in your sleep. Thought maybe there was a boyfriend I didn't know about," she waggled her eyebrows suggestively.

I laughed. "No, definitely not."

She sighed. "Maybe you were dreaming about some hunk. Tristan. That's a good name. Sounds sexy and mysterious."

Shaking my head, still chuckling, I said, "You know I don't dream."

She rolled her eyes. "And as I've said before, everybody dreams. Apparently, you dream about sexy, mysterious men named Tristan."

Typically, to complete Med School takes at least eight years. I was planning to do it in six.

To reach that goal, I took day classes, night classes, summer classes and every kind of class in between. Luckily, after that night of dancing, Isy didn't bother me to go out too much, and that left me with plenty of time to study.

Working at Hearth had a huge advantage, getting hands-on training. And I knew when I got to a point that I could do my residency, Ben would have a position ready for me.

I watched as year after year, more and more students dropped out of the program. There were none that I was friends with, or even particularly friendly. Some unseen force was driving me to get through, and I wouldn't allow anything to stop me.

It was the day after winter break, and I was leaving Hearth to go home and study. Isabel stopped me before I hit the door.

"Wait!" She called out, and as I turned around, Isabel was holding a small gift bag. "I let you get away with not celebrating at 19 and 20, but there's no way I'm letting you get away with the big one."

With a grin, I took the bag from her hand. Inside were three mini bottles of tequila.

"Thanks, Isy. I think I forgot it was my birthday."

Her jaw dropped and she looked personally offended. "Oh, no. No, no, no, I can't have this. You're coming with me."

"Oh, Isy, I really have to…"

Before I could get out a protest, she held up a hand. "You have to what? It's Friday, you're turning 21, and NOTHING. Come on."

She yanked me out the door and brought me to the nearest bar. It was full of college-aged people. There was a small stage with a DJ, strobe lighting and it seemed everyone was celebrating the end of the semester with large quantities of alcohol.

Isabel walked straight to the DJ and to my horror, took his microphone.

"Listen up!" She yelled into it, and everyone gazed up at her. "This here's Reya, and she's legal today! Who wants to buy her a drink?"

While I ducked my head into my hands, I heard a cheer go up in the crowd. Apparently, they liked birthdays, too. Before I knew what was happening, I had a drink in each hand and several requests to chug. I sent my best withering glare at Isabel and obliged them.

At some point, I lost count of the amount of alcohol that had been shoved into my hands. It didn't matter, anyway. Isabel was sticking to me like glue.

"Are you having fun?" She asked me when we found a spot to sit at the bar.

"Actually, I am. Thank you."

The DJ turned over the microphone for karaoke and Isabel started laughing. "We totally have to get up there," she told me.

"Oh, no, no we don't," I denied. I was already out when I had three books to read at home and a 25-page paper to write. What more did she want from me?

Apparently, she wanted me to sing. Against my will, I found myself being dragged onstage, a microphone placed in my hand, and a Shania Twain song blaring over the loud speakers. All the blood raced to my cheeks, and I stood there in a bright red, humiliated coma.

"Uh-oh," I heard Isabel call out. "I think the birthday girl needs some encouragement."

The crowd started a steady beat of clapping and chanting 'sing'. When I looked at Isabel, she was simply grinning, and she began to sing. Since I was refusing to move or speak, Isabel grabbed my hand and began twirling me around the stage. The spinning made me dizzy, and I felt like I was going to lose the little bit of food I had eaten that day. Just in time, Isabel caught the look on my face and held me still without missing a beat on the song. It ended, and I was eternally grateful.

"Come on, let's go sit back down," Isabel said to me, handing off the microphones.

I shot down the stairs and was met by claps on the back. I guess watching someone get close to puking is just as entertaining as watching them sing horribly. With a forced smile to those surrounding me, I turned back to wait for Isabel. She was stepping down from the stage, and the heel of her shoe caught the edge of the step.

With an inward gasp, I pushed my way through the people blocking me and just missed Isabel as she crashed to the floor.

"Isabel!" I called out, and knelt by her side.

She grabbed my hand and I saw tears were ready to spill from her eyes. "Reya, my leg, my leg hurts."

I cut my eyes to the side and saw that there was a bone peeking out from her skin. My mind blanked of everything- the alcohol, the people, the noise. On autopilot, I yelled instructions to anyone close enough to hear.

"Back up! Give me a little space. I need some ice, two towels or shirts and a stack of those chair cushions. And someone call 9-1-1."

Turning my attention back to Isabel, I said, "It's okay, but there is a break on your leg. I'm going to fix you up until help gets here."

She nodded and squeezed my hand. When the ice and towels arrived, I wrapped the ice in one and used the other to secure it to her leg. As gently as possible, I lifted her leg to rest on a stack of cushions when they were brought over. Her gasp of pain tore at me, and I placed both hands on the leg.

Heal quickly, heal strong. What once was one become one again. Fuse, bind and rid what does not belong.

I repeated the chant over and over in my head without conscious thought. Time dropped away, and all that I was aware of was my hands and the leg they rested upon. My eyes were closed, and I could feel warmth creep from my palms into the towels holding the ice. It continued seeping out, drawing from every part of me and focusing on the injury. As the last of the warmth left, blackness enveloped me and I felt myself spinning down, lower and lower until... nothing.

CHAPTER 8

"Tristan! Tristan, something's wrong. I can feel it. What's wrong with me?"

My words were slurred and tinny. I struggled to open my eyes. Tristan's voice was soothing, and I wanted to see him. His arms were wrapped around me and my head rested against his chest. I could feel his heart beat strongly beneath my ear. But something was wrong.

"Reya, come back to me. I'm here. I'll keep you safe. Come back to me now."

I forced my eyes to open and the light immediately stung them. Squeezing them shut, I made a sound between a whimper and a groan.

"Reya, where are you?"

"I'm right here," I heard myself whisper, but the black was sucking me under.

"No, you're not. Where are you? Tell me where you are. I'll come to you. Please, Reya, please..."

"Reya, can you hear me? Reya?"

Words were being whispered through my mind, but I couldn't identify the source. If I could just slip back into the darkness... into the quiet...

"Reya, honey, I need you to open your eyes. Squeeze my hand if you can hear me."

I wanted the darkness back. There were too many layers of fog to sift through. It was holding me down, encouraging me to succumb.

"Oh, God, Reya, please."

There was a buzzing sound now, interfering with the whispers. Buzzing and shrieking. Where was the dark?

"Reya Tane, you open your eyes this minute. I mean it. I'm not messing around."

Someone was groaning in pain. Oh, no, I had to help them. Whoever it was needed my help.

"She's making noise. That's good, right? Reya?"

The sound mingled with the buzzing and whispers, but grew worse. I had to get to them. Only a little more fog. If I could just get out of this fog.

"Where are they?" I wasn't sure if anyone could hear me. My voice sounded gravelly and distant.

"Reya! Oh, thank God, can you open your eyes?"

They opened a slit, and I blinked rapidly to try and clear them. "Isabel? Where are they?"

I could just barely make out her features through the blaring light.

"Where's who, honey?"

"Someone's," I licked my dry lips, "hurt. I can hear them."

I felt a hand tighten on mine. "Reya, it's you. I don't know what happened. Can you tell me if anything hurts?"

Me? I was making those awful noises?

An attempt to shake my head brought me up short. There was something preventing movement. I made a furtive attempt to raise my hand to my face.

They were immediately held down. "Hold on there, Reya. We need to figure out what's wrong first."

It was a man's voice, and I instantly flinched. I didn't recognize it.

"Isabel?" I croaked out.

"It's okay, Reya, we're in an ambulance."

That must be the buzzing noise. It all flashed back to me. Isabel falling, her bone sticking out. So why was I the one being restrained?

"Your... leg."

"Shh," Isabel said. "It was just twisted. I'm fine. We're almost at the hospital now, and Ben's coming too. Can you tell me what hurts?"

The sea of pain was carrying me away, and I only managed to whisper, "Everything."

There was a steady beep resonating through my mind. The fog was back, but not in full force. Keeping my eyes closed, I waited for it to lift. Sounds came first. *Beep, beep.* Voices whispering through a doorway. A toilet flushing. *Beep, beep.*

When I slid my eyes open, I was grateful for the dimly lit room. Two figures sat to the side, and it only took a second for recognition to kick in.

"Isabel. Ben."

Both heads shot up and they crowded the bed. Ben spoke first.

"How are you feeling? Does anything hurt?"

"No," I shook my head lightly. "What happened?"

They glanced at each other. "We're not really sure," Isabel answered first. "We were in that bar, and I fell. Do you remember that?"

I nodded. "You broke your leg."

"Well..." I could hear the hesitation in her voice. "I thought I did. But it's fine now. It hurt a bit at first, but now it doesn't hurt at all."

With narrowed eyes, I studied her. "That doesn't make sense. I saw it."

Isabel looked at Ben again, unsure what to say.

"Reya, the doctors aren't sure what's wrong with you. What else do you remember? Were you feeling anything strange before you passed out?"

"Passed out?" I asked. Closing my eyes again, I did a full body check. Everything seemed fine. Nothing was in pain, only my head hurt a bit. "I feel fine now, just a little groggy," I told Ben.

When I looked back at Isabel, she was chewing on her lower lip. "Look," she burst out, "I have to tell you both this but I don't know what it means. I trust the two of you, but I don't want the other doctors to know." She looked at both of us for confirmation and continued. "When I fell, I thought I had broken my leg. I remember looking down on it and it looked like..." She visibly shuddered before continuing, "The bone was sticking out. Then you put ice on it, so it was cold, but then you had your hands on it and I felt this- heat. It got real hot. And then you passed out, and my leg was fine."

They both looked back at me and I shrugged. "I don't know what happened. All I know is I'm exhausted and I'd like to go home. Can you arrange that, Ben?"

He patted my arm. "Sure thing, sweetheart. I'll be right back."

I waited until he left the room to speak again. "Isy?"

She sat down and rubbed her hand up and down my arm. "Yeah?"

"Don't take this the wrong way, but I don't think we should go out anymore."

Time was passing quickly, and I was on track for my goal. At times I felt, and I'm sure looked, like the walking dead. Most days I didn't eat unless I was reminded to, and I didn't leave any room to dwell on unexplained mysteries.

It was already headed towards summer, with finals approaching and just a few short days in between those and summer school to rest. I would be spending them at Hearth.

When I walked in, I knew it was going to be a hectic day. Isabel was putting three phone calls on hold before she could talk to one, and the waiting room was packed. We had a full staff, and each person was overwhelmed.

My job was sifting through the injured and sick to decide order of importance, plus I got the added bonus of keeping people calm. Doing this job made me realize what a short leash of patience most people possessed. It wasn't often we received emergency patients, but occasionally we were the closest for those not able to get an ambulance.

While I was in the middle of explaining to a mother why her sick child could not be seen before a man with a stab wound, the doors burst open and panic instantly permeated the room.

A man with a tear-streaked face was carrying a small child in his arms. His eyes searched wildly before locking onto me.

"Please! My daughter was hit by a car. You have to help her. You have to save her."

I glanced at Isabel and we shared a moment of grief. "Ben's in surgery, Taylor and Adam are with a gunshot victim," she told me, though I already knew.

My eyes jumped back to the man, and I motioned for him to follow me through the double doors. I found an empty bed in the hall and had him position the girl on her back.

"What exactly happened?" I asked him, already going through the motions of searching for vitals. I knew I could get in huge trouble for this, but I just couldn't leave the little girl in pain.

"We were walking, and I turned my back for just one second and next thing I knew," from the corner of my eye I saw his hands clench together, "she had stepped into the street, and a car hit her. Is she breathing? Tell me she's breathing."

"Sir, I'm going to do my best for her. What's her name?" I spoke in my most reassuring voice, although the girl's pulse was extremely weak, and it didn't look good. From what I could tell, she was struck on the left side, breaking her arm, at least bruising a couple ribs and her knee was twisted out of joint.

"Annabel. Her name is Annabel. Oh, please, help her."

"Okay, I'm going to have you stand on her right," I told him, "I need you to talk to her, try to get her to open her eyes."

He nodded, stood next to her and began murmuring. Her eyes opened for just a brief second and met mine, and I forgot everything else. There was pain, and joy, and innocence in those eyes. She was not afraid, not pleading, but I knew I had to do anything in my power to save her.

My surroundings became fuzzy until the only thing that was clear was the small form lying before me. Slowly, but deliberately, I moved my hands a scant inch above her body. Somewhere in my brain I was registering things I didn't fully understand. After a complete scan, I positioned my hands just above and below her rib cage.

Fluid escaped, be trapped for me. Stitch and seal, find those that flee. Bring them home and heal this girl. Quick and safe, that is my will.

Over and over the words chanted in my head. I felt the warmth building and spread from my palms into her side. When the warmth was gone, I collapsed to the floor.

Two strong arms lifted me to a chair, and the man's face was in front of me. With all my might, I forced my eyes to focus on his face.

"Are you okay?"

I nodded, and stood on wobbly legs. When I took a step back towards the bed, Annabel's eyes were open and gazing at me.

"You still have a couple things to get fixed up, so can you stay real still for me?" When she nodded, I turned towards the father. "It looks like her arm is broken and her knee is twisted. As soon as the doctor is available, I'll have him get her set. She should be fine."

Tears were shining in his eyes as he nodded his head. I turned and found Isabel coming through the doorway. Her eyes were wide and fixed on Annabel. When she looked at me, I motioned towards the office.

Once inside I sank down on a chair and looked up at her. "She's okay."

"What happened?"

"Isy- I- I don't know what to say. How bad is it out there?"

"I grabbed Roger on his way back from lunch. We can spare a minute."

Leaning back in the chair, I stared up at the ceiling. "I know we never talk about that day."

Knowing immediately what I spoke of, she sat down in a chair beside mine. "We don't know what happened."

"Well, whatever it was, I think it just happened again."

"No. Reya, this is crazy."

Bringing my head down to meet her in the eye, I said, "Crazy, yes. But, Isabel," to punctuate my point, I grabbed both her hands and leaned towards her. "There's something inside me. I don't know what it is, I don't know where it came from, but it's there. When I was with that little girl, I knew she was bleeding internally. And I'm willing to bet all my paychecks that Ben will find evidence of it, and it will be almost completely healed. Isabel," I shook her hands when she began shaking her head, "I know I can help people. Maybe that's why I've felt so driven to get through school."

"But if what happened to you the night you..." She gestured towards her leg. "I just can't watch you go through that again. You scared me, Reya."

There was utter sincerity in her eyes. I nodded my understanding, but pressed on. "But it didn't happen this time. Listen. I felt more... controlled. And I did collapse afterwards, but I didn't black out, and I stood right back up. I think with practice..."

"Absolutely not. You don't even know what it is!"

"I have to try. I saved that little girl's life today. I know I did. Isabel, I have to try." My tone left no room for discussion.

She searched my face for a long time before nodding. "We better get back out there."

Standing, I stopped at the door and looked back at her. "Could we keep this quiet for now? I mean, not even Ben."

"Sure. The less people the better, in my mind." But she smiled, and I knew my secret was safe.

CHAPTER 9

For the last ten minutes, I had been staring at my reflection in the mirror. It was over. Done. *Finito*. I was officially a Med School graduate.

The image staring back at me looked young, but confident. I *was* young, by all means, to be a resident, but physically I could still pass for a high school student. In my life, there was no significant other, no wild parties and certainly not a lot of sleep. But I was where I wanted to be. With everything in me, I knew I was meant to help people, and now I had the opportunity.

Shaking myself out of my reverie, I headed off to my first official day as a resident at Hearth.

The days were typical, steady and fulfilling. There wasn't a lot of cheat room on the years of residency; I was looking at four before I could apply for a medical license. Ben took me under his wing, as he had since the beginning, and I spent each spare minute continuing my studies. It seemed never ending.

Only occasionally did I allow my other skills to surface. The more practice I had with the residency, the easier the other skills became. Instead of analyzing them to death, I simply accepted it as a sixth sense. Even if I wanted to, where would I go to find out more information? Was there a website for paranormal healing? Actually, there probably was.

As soon as my resident term was complete, I applied for and received a medical license.

"So," Isabel commented, watching me hang it up in the office. "You've met your goal. Now what are you going to do?"

I looked over at her with a smile. "Work, of course."

"Well, Dr. Tane, I hope not too hard. I need you as a maid of honor in September."

My eyes grew wide and I jumped into her arms. "I can't believe it! You're getting married?"

She nodded, grinning from ear to ear. "Matt proposed over the weekend. I know September is in just two months, but it just feels right. So, you'll be my maid of honor?"

"Yes, of course I will. I'm so excited for you. Matt's a great guy. You two will be happy."

Everything seemed the same. The grass was green, the air was clean, the water was clear. But for some reason there was a quickness to my step, my eyes darted back and forth though I couldn't figure out what I was searching for. My heart was thudding in my chest, and terror gripped me. Faster I moved, away from the stream and into the woods until I was sprinting through the foliage.

And then I spotted him. Tristan. He was lying in a heap under a canopy of trees. My heart was beating so hard it was threatening to jump out. At a straight out sprint I got to his side and rolled him to his back.

"Tristan? Can you hear me?"

He opened his eyes and the dark obsidian met mine. "You came."

His voice was low and tired. It felt as if a vice gripped my heart.

"Of course, I did. What happened to you?" Even as I asked, I glanced down and saw the blood. "Oh, no, what happened?"

"It's nothing. A scratch."

Even with the gravity of the situation, I rolled my eyes. "Is that a guy thing? Come on, I'll fix you."

He shook his head and winced in pain. "How?"

"Are you kidding? This is a dream. Lay down on that bed over there," I gestured behind me and sure enough, a bed appeared. "And I'll see what's wrong."

With my arm under his, I helped lift him and walk the few feet towards the bed. Though he made no sound, I could see the pain on his face.

"Leave me. You have to leave me. They can't find you."

"Oh, shut up. I'm fixing you, and you're going to get better." His eyes drifted closed, and I feared he was unconscious. Well, at least he would stop bothering me.

I got to work. The main cut was nasty, but when I opened his shirt I saw there were similar, shallower cuts crisscrossing along his chest and onto his back. It bothered me more than any other injury ever had. Without hesitating, I put my hands over the worst one and focused.

The knowledge was swiftly followed by the heat. Within seconds, he was healing. When I opened my eyes, he was staring intently at me. He took my hands lightly in his and spoke.

"You healed me."

"I told you I would."

"Thank you."

"You should rest with injuries like these, macho man."

Tristan closed his eyes, but a small grin played over his lips. He still hadn't relinquished control over my hands. They felt small, frail, and, most surprisingly, safe, inside his.

"I've been looking for you, you know." His voice was still rough, but loads better than when I first found him in a heap on the ground.

"Well, it looks like you found me. Are you going to give me my hands back?"

Popping his eyes open, he grinned wide. "Am I making you nervous?"

My heart actually skipped a beat. Good thing this was a dream, because stuff like that wasn't supposed to happen in real life.

"Of course not," I said, tugging inconsequentially at my hands.

"What are you doing?" He asked, peering down at my struggling hands.

With an exaggerated sigh, I told him, "Trying to get my hands back."

"Hmm." He murmured, staring down at our joined hands before switching his gaze to my face. Or, more specifically, my mouth. Suddenly, I was very much aware of the large, soft bed I had conjured to heal him.

"Hmm, what?"

"I'm thinking. There could be a way to let go of your hands."

Rolling my eyes, I asked the obvious. "What would that be?"

His eyes jumped to mine. "You'll have to trust me."

"Yeah, sure, I trust you," I said half-heartedly.

The smile turned smug and my heart jumped again.

"I'm glad to hear it," he murmured, carefully pressing a kiss into each of my palms. Slowly, he released my hands and took hold of my face.

My eyes went wide as I realized his intention, but I made no move to stop him. His lips pressed gently against mine and I sank into absolute bliss.

It was the first time he had kissed me. It was everything I could have ever imagined and more. The world spun out until all that remained was Tristan, his lips pressing softly against mine and his hands cupping my face.

I felt my heart speed out of control and my body respond in a way I hadn't realized was possible. Giving in to the feeling, the moment, I tangled my fingers into the long, silky fall of his hair.

His mouth became more urgent, though it remained gentle as the lapping waves on the shore. He rolled until his body pressed its weight into mine. Of their own accord, my arms wrapped him closer and my body arched into his, needing, craving the contact.

Hands explored and inhibitions were forgotten. I became almost frantic with a need I didn't recognize, or understand.

His hands closed around my wrists, pinning them to the bed. His head lifted and those dark eyes met mine.

"Do you give yourself to me, tau o te ate?"

"Yes. Yes, Tristan. I'm yours."

I was running down the dock in three-inch heels, cursing myself for not wearing my normal tennis shoes and changing into the torture shoes later. There were two men dressed in tuxedos standing to each side of the loading plank, grinning at me.

"I'm here! Oh, shoot, I have that invitation somewhere," I began, but put a palm against my forehead when my abrupt stop had it spinning. After a moment, it cleared and I frantically began digging through my bag.

"It's okay, I recognize the dress. Go on in," one of them said.

"Thanks!" I called out as I dashed onto the boat.

Following the directions Isabel had given me the previous day, I rushed to the lower deck and down a hallway. I flew into the last room with apologies on the tip of my tongue.

"Told you she would be late," Isabel said when I entered. "Probably out saving lives."

"Oh, leave her alone," an older woman with graying hair good-humoredly tapped Isabel's shoulder. "She's just on time. Come on in, dear. I'm Isabel's mother, Marie. So nice to finally meet you."

There were two other women in the room- Susie, I had already met, was the other bridesmaid, and another woman with short, spiky hair was eyeing me disdainfully.

"Such beautiful hair, such a waste. Sit," the woman ordered, pointing at a chair.

I glanced helplessly at Isabel but she merely smiled. "Darlene is the stylist my mom surprised me with. She's going to do all of our hair and make-up today, which is a good thing since I see you simply rolled out of bed before arriving."

Rolling my eyes, I took a seat. "Didn't want to out-shine you on your wedding day," I told her.

We shared a smile before I was under Darlene's mercy.

An excruciating hour later, I was standing with Isabel, watching as her little cousin made her way down the aisle. I pressed a hand to my suddenly queasy stomach.

"Are you all right?" Isabel whispered to me.

Nodding, I managed a smile back at her. "You'd think I'm the one getting married. Don't worry," I said, attempting to be reassuring.

Susie stepped onto the aisle, and then it was my turn. When I reached the front, I shot a quick smile at Matt before turning to watch Isabel make her entrance.

The ceremony was beautiful, the boat sailing through Boston Harbor at sunset. Once vows were said and the hoots and hollers had quieted from Matt's enthusiastic kiss for the bride, the chairs were scooted off to the side and tables were brought out. Dinner was served and the dance floor was left open in anticipation of the bride and groom's first dance.

At the head table, I sat to Isabel's left and waited for the dreaded speech. Public speaking was not one of my fortes. Inevitably, the clinking of glasses signaled it was my time.

I stood quickly and the motion made my head spin, again. For a split second my vision blurred and went dark, but I took a deep breath and managed not to fall over. A glance at Isabel told me the action didn't go unnoticed.

Clearing my throat, I smiled and began my speech. "What can I say about love? It is one of those unfathomable and indefinable things that has been argued and pined over for centuries. No one really knows why, or how it happens. But when it does," I paused, looking down at the beaming Isabel. "It changes you for all time. For better or worse, once love has a hold of you it doesn't let go. Personally, I never understood it. Never thought about it. Until that day when Isabel told me she found the one, the one she was meant to spend the rest of her life with. That day, I looked into her eyes, and I saw. I saw what love was, and how it completes two people. I understood those poems and movies, because in that moment, I knew that Isabel and Matt could conquer all. True love, the kind they have found with each other, is truly a completing of two souls. Infallible, indispensable and inseparable. Congratulations, Mr. and Mrs. Beauford." I raised my glass in a toast, and everyone followed suit. Grateful I was done, I sat back down.

Isabel leaned over to whisper, "Didn't know you had it in you, you big softie."

"Don't worry, I stole most of it from an old episode of *The Love Boat*."

Isabel stifled a laugh and turned to listen attentively to the other speeches.

As they went on, I picked half-heartedly through my food. Though I hadn't eaten all day, I had no appetite.

Isabel leaned close to me again once they were finished. "Does the food taste okay?"

"Yeah, it's wonderful. Guess it's all those nerves," I smiled and patted her arm. "Giving my little girl away," I faked a sniffle.

She snorted gracefully and said, "Right. *Your* little girl. My mom's dancing a jig, she never thought I'd get hitched."

"Well, at least she likes Matt. I can't quite imagine her being one of those awful mother-in-law's."

"You've never seen her when someone's late to dinner. Never mess with an Italian woman and her kitchen," she warned with a grin.

"I'll keep that in mind," I answered.

After dinner and quite a few dances, Ben grabbed me and led me to the dance floor. His wife was dancing happily with Matt, flushed from the wine.

"She seems to be having a good time," I commented.

"Belle of the ball, my Teresa." He studied me for a moment before continuing. "How are you feeling?"

"Me? I'm fine."

"You didn't look fine when you stood for your speech. And you hardly ate anything."

I sent Isabel a quick glare. "Tattle-tale."

Ben laughed. "She didn't have to tell me. I am your doctor, after all. And in all the time I've known you, I've never seen you sick. If you're still feeling poorly in a couple days, I want you to have a check-up."

Groaning, I said, "I'm fine."

Laughing again, Ben said, "Typical doctor, you don't like doctors yourself. I'm sure it's nothing serious, but it will put my mind at ease. Promise me?"

With a sigh, I nodded. There wasn't much I wouldn't do for Ben, even if that meant being put under the microscope.

The party lasted well into the night, and I made sure to act as normal as possible. I didn't want anything to ruin Isabel's day.

When the boat docked, we sent them off with a happy farewell. They were going to spend the night in a suite at the Four Season's before heading off to Aruba for a week. I drove home and sank happily into bed.

I awoke at 5:00 in the morning and raced to the bathroom. When my stomach was empty, I sank back on my heels and put my head in my hands. How could I be sick? I don't get sick. The flu was going around, but it was always going around.

After a few minutes on the floor, I felt better and stood to rinse my face and mouth. No longer tired, I went to the kitchen and made myself some light herbal tea. Taking small sips, I headed to the backyard and watched as the sun slowly peeked above the horizon. When it touched the reds and golds of fall, the view was breathtaking.

I dressed and headed into Hearth as usual. The tea had helped soothe my stomach, and even though I felt better, I hadn't dared food yet. I was just hoping to get through the day.

The morning went by with no glitches. Around lunchtime, I walked into the back office to grab a file and was met by the smell of Chinese take-out. Roger and Gary were hiding out, eating their lunch while going over reports. As the smell hit me, I felt myself pale and my stomach drop. Without so much as a word, my hand covered my mouth and I ran.

Since I hadn't eaten anything, there wasn't much to come back up. For the second time that day, I rinsed my face and mouth and stared at myself in the mirror. My face was paler than normal and my eyes had heavy bags beneath them. I placed one hand over my stomach and closed my eyes. There was just too much to do, I couldn't afford to be sick.

When I opened the door, I came face to face with Ben. He looked stern and simply pointed towards an exam room. Shoulders hunched, I led the way and sat down.

Ben sat opposite me after shutting the door. "Tell me your symptoms," he said.

I squirmed like a child with her hand caught in the cookie jar. "Dizziness, nausea and lack of appetite."

"How long?"

"The day before the wedding I felt dizzy a couple times, mostly when I stood up fast. The nausea mostly yesterday, and I've thrown up twice today. I never have much of an appetite, but it was the worst yesterday and today."

Ben was nodding, taking notes on a clipboard. "How have you been sleeping?"

I shrugged. "Nothing abnormal." He gave me a look and I expanded. "Not very well. Tossing and turning at night, and I've been tired during the day. That's been for a couple weeks or so."

He studied me and asked a question that made my stomach flip. "When was your last menstrual cycle?"

The blood rushed to my cheeks, but quickly drained when I counted back. "Six weeks ago," I whispered.

"Was there anything abnormal about it?"

"I- I don't know. I mean… I don't really pay attention to that sort of thing."

"Reya, have you ever been late before?"

I shook my head. "No. No, Ben, I know where you're going with this, but it can't be. I… well, I've never…" Embarrassed again, I stared down at the floor. "I'm a virgin," I admitted quietly.

Ben's brows creased, and he stood. "I'll be right back," he said.

I sat staring at my feet with my head reeling. I hadn't even formed a coherent thought before Ben came back into the room with an ultrasound.

"Lay back for me," he said calmly.

I did, shaking my head. "This is a waste of time, Ben. I can't be."

"We'll just rule it out, then," he said and lifted my shirt to expose my stomach.

As patiently as possible, I waited for the test to come back negative so I could get on with my day. Then, faintly but undoubtedly, the flutter of a tiny heartbeat filled the room.

CHAPTER 10

Present Day

"Tristan," I whispered.

Those dark, fathomless eyes changed almost imperceptibly, going from smoldering to just slightly wary. They narrowed, as if he were trying to see through me.

With my free hand, I smoothed a strand of hair from his face. Though he didn't flinch from the contact, he still held a death grip on my other wrist.

"Reya! I'm so sorry, I shouldn't have let you in here. Please, let me get someone, we'll get him off you, I should have known better."

I simply held up a hand to cut off Aden's rambling. Holding Tristan's gaze with mine, I continued soothing him like I would a frightened animal. Because in this moment, a frightened animal was exactly what he was. Frightened, and ready to fight.

"Do you know me, Tristan? There's a place that we meet. A secret place, only you and I know about. It's beautiful there, with soft green grass and trees swaying above. Birds are always humming a tune, and there's a lovely river that's warm no matter the time of year."

I kept my voice soft and consistent. One by one, his fingers relaxed their grip and the blood rushed back to my hand.

"That's the way. You see, you remember me. I didn't know you were here, but I know now. And I swear, I will get you out of here. You hear me? I will get you out."

As an answer, his eyes closed and his head slumped once again. My heart that had been in my throat suddenly dropped to my stomach.

"Aden, I want you to stay as far away as possible. No matter what happens, don't come close enough for him to reach you. Understand?" Glancing over my shoulder, I saw him staring at me through wide eyes. He nodded and I turned back to Tristan.

I ran my hands over every square inch of his body, healing as I went. The energy poured into me like I'd never felt before. Without question, I simply used it to heal every scratch and intrusion I came across, no matter how small. When it was complete, I placed my hands gently on his head.

"Sleep to heal that which cannot be easily fixed."

Satisfied I had done everything in my power, I stood and faced Aden.

"We better get back before you're in any sort of trouble." Not waiting for his reply, I merely stepped out of the tent and began the walk back.

There was no weakness in me now. It had been replaced with a boiling fury that knew no bounds. Aware of that, I did my best to keep it on a low simmer.

Aden easily matched my pace but remained silent on our brisk walk back. As soon as we ducked inside, Aden broke the silence.

"You knew him."

"Not exactly."

"What do you mean, not exactly? You called him by name."

"I know that."

"SO HOW DO YOU KNOW HIM?"

"Hush," I admonished. "I doubt it would do either of us good to have this conversation overheard."

"He responded to you," he continued, quieter, but without missing a beat.

"Yes."

"Well?"

I glanced over at Aden, who was standing hands on hips with an exasperated look.

I sighed. "He's the father of my child."

Silence. Then, "WHAT?"

"Aden!" I hissed sharply.

"How can you drop something like that and not expect me to yell?" He asked quieter, but with just as much intensity.

I sank to the floor and rested my head in my hands. "I hardly understand it myself." Inside, deep down, I was still shaking with fear and anger. But, more than anything, determination.

Aden sat beside me and waited for me to speak again.

"You've seen and heard unbelievable things, so I'm going to tell you about this and hope you won't think I'm insane."

He remained silent, which I took to be an affirmative. "I lost my parents before I could even remember them. I grew up in a state program, and didn't have many friends. Actually, I didn't have any. My whole focus was on school, and learning as much as possible. It wasn't a great life, but it wasn't bad, either. I used to imagine a place, a place that was solely mine, that no one could watch me or tell me what to do. It was beautiful, always warm with giant trees and a soothing river."

Shaking my head, I shrugged. "At least I thought I imagined it. I would dream about it, at night. But when I awoke in the morning, I never remembered the dream. Then, one day, there was someone else in the dream with me."

"Tristan," Aden murmured.

I nodded. "Tristan. But it was the same- not once did I ever remember the dream when I woke up. When I saw him in that tent, when I looked into his eyes, everything came back to me. Hundreds of memories, of time spent together in this made-up place." Facing Aden again, I grabbed his hands. "Somehow, those dreams were not just dreams. Somehow, what we shared in that forest was actually real. I know it, down to my soul. A couple months ago, I found him in the dream, and he had those same marks on him that he has now. I healed him in the dream."

"You know this sounds crazy," Aden said.

"I know."

"And yet I believe you."

A smile turned up the corners of my mouth. "Thank you."

He sighed and shoved a hand through his hair. "Great," he muttered. "You've gone and torn up my conscious."

"No," I said firmly. "You're a good man, Aden. That's why I got into the cab with you, and that's why I've shared this with you. You may have had something awful happen, but it doesn't change who you are inside. So now, I'm going to ask for your help."

His hands rubbed his face now, and at length he looked up. "All right."

"Thank you, again. And, Aden, I promise you this. Once we're out of here, I will do everything in my power to help you find out what happened to your sister. And the men who hurt her."

Tears sprung to his eyes, which he ruthlessly blinked back. He nodded and stood. "I best be getting your meal. They'll think something's wrong. I'll have to tie you up again, for appearance sake."

I nodded and scooted closer to the pole. He worked quickly and left, calling a guard to the opening. My mind was racing, trying to devise a plan. If only I had spent more time watching James Bond and less time reading books.

Then, a thought struck.

Digging through my bag, I desperately wanted a change of clothes, but even more importantly, I was searching for my hair ties. After shimmying into a new pair of jeans, which were getting just a bit snug, I performed a happy dance. Thank goodness, I had packed bobby pins.

We waited another week and a half. I ate, healed and slept. Aden only spent a few hours with me as my babysitter, in hopes that Donovan wouldn't suspect anything. During those few hours, we planned our strategy.

The morning we were going to put our plan in motion, I changed into the darkest pair of blue jeans I had and a black, long sleeved shirt. I shoved my license and passport into my pockets, along with the cash I had. The rest of the clothes would have to stay.

Aden came in at dusk. "He's gone," he reported.

"Okay, good. Let's do this."

Donovan left, and would be gone for three days. It was our best chance.

We walked out of the tent as normal, Aden leading me by the arm. With my head down I followed him, afraid my expression would give me away. We paused outside the only guarded tent, and after a nod of approval, stepped inside. Without pause to take in the fresh abuse, I knelt in front of Tristan and pulled a pin from my hair.

"Tristan, we're getting you out. Can you hear me? We're getting you out."

He was unresponsive, and I focused on my task. I just prayed it would work.

Snapping the bobby pin in half, I took the side with a slight curve and inserted it into the lock. A little jimmy, and nothing happened.

"Is it working?" Aden whispered beside me.

"Shoot. No. Give me a second." I tried again. Laying the pin flat, the curve stuck into the key hole, I slowly lifted it. With a slight click, the cuff came loose.

A huge smile covered my face as I lifted it to Aden. Quickly I performed the same trick on his other wrist. It worked, and I slipped them off. Next was the pillory, which had a simple lock holding the top and bottom together. It took a bit longer, but I managed to unlock it. Only his feet were left.

Aden lifted the wooden trap while I disengaged the leg irons. As soon as his legs were free, Tristan grabbed Aden by the throat.

I stifled a gasp and rushed to step between the two men. One hand, I placed on the arm restraining Aden; the other, I placed on Tristan's chest.

"Tristan." I kept my voice calm, even while I could sense the breath leaving Aden's body. "Look at me, Tristan. He's a friend. He's helping us. Please, do this for me. Let him go."

His eyes flicked to me, and I understood Aden's original description of him. *Raw power.*

"Let him go, Tristan. Your fight is not with him. We have to leave now. Please."

In a sudden move, he relaxed his hand and Aden collapsed to the floor. Leaning down, I checked his vitals only to find myself hauled back to my feet. Tristan swept me behind him and was in a fighting stance, his eyes focused on Aden.

"Oh, for heaven's sake." I pulled gently at Tristan's arm, fearful for Aden. Tristan shot his heated gaze at me, and I met fire with fire. "Is this how you treat friends? I need to help him, and then we all need to get out of here."

Tristan didn't budge. With an inward sigh, I stepped closer. "He won't hurt me," I murmured to him, "And he won't take me from you. I'm yours, you hear me? I'm yours. Now let me help him."

Keeping my eyes on Tristan, I moved around him and next to Aden. Still watching Tristan, I spread my hands out to make sure Aden was still alive. Carefully, I placed my hands on his throat and cleared his passageway. He coughed and sat up.

Just as slowly, I stood and walked back to Tristan. Only when I placed a hand inside his did I look back at Aden. "We have to go now," I said quietly. He nodded, glancing warily at Tristan. Tristan's hard gaze stayed steady.

At the back left corner, Aden hefted out the spike holding the tent down and motioned us to slip under. Allowing him to lead the way, I kept my hand firmly in Tristan's.

We ran in a half crouch away from the camp. There were guards circling the camp, but Aden had done his homework. At a break in the line we slipped through and found ourselves in the middle of the desert.

"There's a dry ravine where we can find cover, and follow it into the next town," Aden whispered as he motioned towards his right. I nodded and we followed him at a quick pace.

Just as we were reaching the edge of the ravine, there was a crackle of a radio. We froze and hit the ground, but could clearly hear the warning.

"There's been an escape, repeat, there's been an escape. Close the perimeter."

In the darkness, I could just make out the outline of a guard. He spun at the command with a weapon in his hand. I'm surprised he didn't hear my heart pounding. We watched silently as he crept past us, not three feet away. Patiently we waited until Aden motioned us forward.

We slid into the ravine and crept along, Aden at our flank. It was black as pitch and difficult to see, even though I searched frantically around. Only a few minutes passed before I heard the inevitable voice behind us.

"Stop where you are."

CHAPTER 11

I twisted around and found myself once again shoved behind Tristan. Aden was being held with an arm around his throat and a gun to his head.

"Wait, please!" I called out, and the gun swung to me.

"Women. Nothing but trouble. I may as well shoot you."

At once, Tristan leaped and Aden spun. Blocked as I was by Tristan's back, I couldn't see what exactly transpired. It only lasted a second before I saw the guard stumble back, a scream tearing through his throat. It was dark, but I could have sworn I saw dark red streaks across his face.

"Run!" I heard Aden yell.

As I turned to do so, Tristan grabbed up my hand and yanked me forward. None of us looked back, running several miles until I felt as if my lungs were being torn from my chest. Instead of allowing me to slow, Tristan simply swept me into his arms. It felt comforting and incredibly ridiculous, but I knew better than to open my mouth.

From our earlier discussions, I knew the nearest town was 15 miles away. After catching my breath, I motioned for Tristan to set me down, and we continued at a jog towards the town. It took a couple hours to reach it. When the lights of the town were visible, we slowed to a walk.

It was amazing to me that Tristan was even on his feet. As we moved swiftly through the village, I put aside the questions that were on the tip of my tongue and kept moving.

The town was no more than a small village, with a few scattered houses and a row of stores. There was an inn, but we knew if Donovan's men came looking, it would be the first place they checked. With my hand locked in Tristan's, I felt him begin to sag. I glanced over at Aden with panic.

He seemed to understand. "Just through town there's an abandoned house we should be able to stay in for the night. We can take turns as lookouts, and we'll leave before the light."

I nodded and picked up the pace, worried for Tristan. We should have stopped so I could examine him. Why did I let him carry me? I should have pushed myself.

As if reading my thoughts, he squeezed my hand gently so that I looked up at him. His features were so dark he nearly disappeared in the night. When our eyes met, I felt my stomach give a little jump.

Turning back to the path, I followed Aden up a small hill and saw the tiny structure that would be our hotel for the night. It looked as if it could fall down any moment, but there were no neighbors so we shouldn't be noticed.

A front window was broken, and Aden used it to gain entrance. Inside, there was a kitchen, a living room and a back bedroom and bath. The water wouldn't be working, unfortunately, but I led Tristan to the bedroom and laid him on the floor. Aden followed me in but hung back.

"I'll take first watch, Reya."

"Wake me in a few hours, Aden. You'll need some sleep too."

He nodded and stepped back into the living room. Sitting beside Tristan, I did a quick examination and healed what I could. When I looked up, his eyes were watching me.

"You need to rest," I told him.

He blinked and continued to stare at me. I sighed and lay beside him. "All right, I do, too." With one hand, I smoothed away his hair. He trapped my hand and laid it across his chest, above his heart. His other hand eased my head to his shoulder before curling around my waist. Within moments I was out.

I felt the light nudging and struggled out of the darkness. At once, recent events flooded my mind and I snapped my eyes open, expecting the worst.

"Reya, it's a couple hours 'til dawn."

Aden was on the opposite side of me from Tristan, and he looked exhausted. Carefully, I untangled myself from Tristan's arm and scooted out.

"You should have woken me sooner," I admonished him when I stepped back into the living room.

"You need sleep more than I do. And he does more than either of us," he said, motioning towards Tristan.

"I know. I'm glad you understood that." I sat by the broken window and looked out. "It's quiet here," I commented.

"Yeah. I'm going to sleep out here, so you can wake me if you need anything."

I nodded. "Aden, about the baby- can we just keep it quiet for a while?

With a sharp nod, he dropped to the floor and immediately fell asleep.

Turning back to the window, I let my thoughts drift. Just two and a half weeks ago, I was living a completely normal life, watching my best friend get married. Now, I was a hostage escapee with a child conceived in her dreams. How quickly life can turn bizarre.

As the sky began to lighten, I woke Aden. He hadn't gotten nearly enough sleep, but it couldn't be helped at this point.

"Where to from here?" I asked.

"We've got to get as far away as possible. The only problem will be if we use any sort of identification, Donovan will be able to track us. So I was thinking…"

"New Zealand."

We both turned at the new voice, and I felt my heart rate quicken when I met those dark eyes. They were focused entirely on me.

"New Zealand?" Aden finally asked.

"Yes. I have a home there. It will be safe." While he spoke, his eyes never left mine.

"How will we get there?" I asked.

"By boat. We must find a way to Sydney. We will be able to get on a boat without ID."

Aden and I glanced at each other. If we were lucky, it would take at least a few days to reach Sydney, and who knew how long to arrive in New Zealand. But, with lack of a better plan, it was decided.

My eyes met Tristan's again, a strange fire spreading from the tips of my toes out through the top of my head. When he spoke, his eyes remained on mine.

"Aden, I apologize for my actions last night. I was not myself."

"Oh, uh, it's fine," Aden spluttered.

"Would you mind giving us a moment alone?" Tristan asked next.

"Sure thing. I'll make a sweep of the town before we head out for supplies."

Aden took his leave, and I remained rooted to the spot. My heart was hammering in my chest as I took in the man from my dreams, the father of my child.

His dark eyes never left mine. *Why do you look so skittish*, tau o te ate?

I jumped, as the words were not spoken aloud but inside my head.

"How did you..?" my voice trailed off, awed at his obvious abilities.

He took one step forward, and though I realized it was childish, I took a step back. He paused again, watching me curiously.

You can do the same, he spoke in my mind.

Shaking my head in denial, I backed up once more only to find myself up against the wall.

You have no idea of your true powers, do you?

"Please, stop," I begged, squeezing my eyes shut.

His hand was suddenly stroking the side of my face, though just a moment ago he'd been across the room. My eyes shot open, but any question that had been on my lips was immediately cut off by the look in his eyes.

"Reya," he spoke aloud now, his voice just a faint whisper of sound. The rough velvet caressed my skin. "I have been searching for you for a long time," he told me.

"I don't... I don't really understand what's happening."

He looked confused now. "What do you mean?"

"Tristan, I..." Trailing off, I closed my eyes, shaking my head to clear the cobwebs. Focusing back on him, I continued. "The dreams I had, I never remembered them. Until I saw you, in real life, chained up in that tent," I paused again, choking up at the memory. "I didn't know who you were, didn't have any memory of you, until that moment."

Tristan thought through this. "That is actually a bit relieving," he finally said.

My questioning look was all the prompting he needed to continue.

"When we first began meeting in our dreams, I believed I made you up. It wasn't until the night you were injured that I realized you were real. I've been searching for you since then."

"That was years ago," I whispered, completely bewildered.

"Yes," he took slow steps towards me. Though I swallowed hard, I kept my ground this time. "I couldn't understand why you would not come to me, why you were closed off to me." He was within a foot now, and his hand reached out to my face again. "There were many times I thought I was wrong, that you were not my mate. But now, with you here, your memories returned and the fact I can reach you in your mind, I know I was not mistaken."

"Your... your mate?" I practically squeaked out.

His smile was slow and sexy. Leisurely, he moved closer to me until our lips were just a hairsbreadth apart. "You are my mate, my other half. I know it now more than ever."

His voice skittered across my skin and I found myself reaching out to him, both my body and my mind.

Mine, I whispered into his mind as our lips touched. It was the gentlest of kisses, yet it started my entire body aflame.

There was a light tapping on the door and we broke apart, but I could still feet the impression of his lips against mine.

To be continued later, he promised inside my mind.

I nodded once, then turned to open the door after checking through the window that it was, indeed, Aden.

"It's all clear. Nothing seems out of place," Aden informed us.

"We should gather some supplies at the store," I told them, "enough to get us to Sydney."

They both nodded and we headed out. A general store was just opening up, and I started inside. Tristan made his own sweep along the street while Aden stayed out front, always watching for Donovan's guards.

I smiled at the clerk and gathered items that would keep for a few days traveling. At the counter, I dumped an armful of mostly granola bars and water. There wasn't a very wide selection. Near the check stand, I found a bag that would make carrying the items a bit easier, and added it to the pile.

Hunkered down by my goodies, I stepped outside and blinked into the sun that had risen completely. Aden was on alert, but Tristan wasn't back yet. We shoved all the stuff into the bag, and just as we were zipping it, I glanced up and met the eyes of a man staring back at me from across the street. It wasn't one of Donovan's guards, from what I could tell. After a moment, he stepped into the street and started straight for me.

"Aden," I whispered, but the man was quick.

"Who are you?" He demanded, stepping onto the walk.

I opened my mouth to answer, but Aden stepped between us. "Hey now," he began, but the man completely ignored him and approached me. Grabbing my arm, he looked at me closely.

"I said, who are you?" He had amber eyes and dark brown hair streaked with red, much like my own.

Behind me, a sound that could only be described as a growl erupted and I found myself once again thrust backwards.

"Tristan," this time it wasn't me, but the newcomer that breathed the name. "Tristan, is it really you?"

Still in a fighting crouch, Tristan didn't respond. The man didn't seem to notice.

"Oh, thank God, you're all right. I've been searching for you, I thought…" He trailed off, seeming to remember me, and noticing Aden for the first time.

"And just who are you?" Aden asked through gritted teeth.

The man flicked his gaze from Tristan's unwavering one and back to Aden. "My name is Jared. And you are?"

"It doesn't seem Tristan recognizes you, *Jared*, so you may just want to step back."

Just about at my wits end with male arrogance, I shoved my way to the middle. Ignoring Aden and Jared, I turned and looked at Tristan.

"Tristan, do you know this man? I have pretty good radar, and I don't sense any ill will. So, I need you to tell me, do we leave him here or hear him out?"

The absolute silence was deafening. From the corner of my eye I noticed the shopkeeper staring at us through the window, and I could only imagine how the scene would look to a passerby.

Suddenly, Tristan's eyes softened and he whispered, "Jared."

The tension melted from the scene. Relief washed through me as I turned back to Jared, still blocking Tristan's path. Casually I linked my hand with his, showing solidarity. Jared took that in but was smart enough not to comment.

"Perhaps we could go somewhere more private," he said instead. "It seems we all have some stories to tell."

CHAPTER 12

Back to the deserted house we went. I fervently hoped there was no over-anxious realtor coming to look at it today.

The four of us stood facing each other in silence. Tristan's hand was still held securely in mine, for I knew somehow that I was his anchor. I was worried about his mental health; first, his attack on Aden, and now, his memory loss concerning Jared. If only I had found out what types of drugs they were using at that infernal camp.

Jared cleared his throat. "I guess I'll begin. Tristan, you've spent the majority of the last five years searching for something," his eyes flicked to me and back again. "It was normal for you to be gone for months at a time, but you always kept in contact with me. When I didn't receive word from you for two weeks, I began looking for you. That was a little over two months ago. The last time we spoke you were in Sydney, so I started there and tracked you to here."

Aden glanced over at the silent Tristan and picked up the story. "Tristan was captured by a man named Donovan Barbury. He's been held captive at a camp about 15 miles from here. As far as I know, its existence is unknown to anyone outside."

Jared glanced over at me. With a shrug, I said, "I flew into Ayers Rock and was kidnapped. I'm a doctor, and they wanted me to help those being tortured." The baby and my healing powers, I figured, were best left alone for the moment.

Jared looked back at Aden. "Were you being held there also?"

Shifting uncomfortably, Aden shook his head. "No. I was working for Donovan."

A low warning slipped from Jared's throat and he crouched, similar to Tristan's initial reaction. Quickly holding up a hand, I interrupted before a fight broke out. "He's with us, Jared. He realized what was happening was wrong, and he helped us escape. Please, hear him out."

Jared relaxed his stance, but was still very much on alert.

Aden used the pause to explain. "My sister was taken by a group of men. They injured me and took her. When I came to, Donovan was there and told me he was after the same people, so I joined forces. At first, I followed him because I believed what he was doing was right. But when Reya came," he held out his hands palms up, "it made me realize that he was wrong." He shook his head, ashamed at himself. When he straightened, his eyes had turned cold and fierce. "But believe me, I will find who took my sister. And they will pay."

Something in Aden's voice relaxed Jared completely. Odd, because the look in his eyes sent a shiver down my spine.

"What do you know about the men who took your sister?"

Aden glanced at me, and I smiled for encouragement. He sighed. "We were in a forest in New Zealand. While we were walking, these huge shadows swooped down, but I couldn't find anything- like a plane or birds- that made them. When I called her back to me, these men appeared out of nowhere. One put his hands on my chest, and I collapsed. When I came to, they were gone."

I had been watching Aden, but when I switched my attention back to Jared, his face had paled. "You saw these shadows?"

Aden ran a hand through his hair. "Yeah. I realize it sounds crazy, and you don't have to believe me. But I know what I saw."

"On the contrary. I believe you completely. It's just that..." His gaze shifted to Tristan, who stood silent during the entire exchange. I glanced up at him as well, and saw him nod.

"He's Gifted." Tristan stated it so simply, so matter of fact, there was no room for argument. Except that I had no clue what he was talking about.

"What?" Aden and I asked simultaneously.

Jared paced to the window and back again, shaking his head and rubbing his jaw. "That means it's worse than I imagined. His sister must be too, that's why they took her. They probably didn't realize what he was, otherwise they would have taken him too."

"He's what?" I repeated, as Aden simultaneously asked, "I'm what?"

"You're gifted. Incredible. And you're a healer, aren't you?" Jared directed this last at me. "This is fantastic." He seemed lost in his own world, still pacing back and forth.

"WHAT ARE YOU TALKING ABOUT?" My shout finally caught his attention.

"Yes, right, sorry. Aden here has the potential to become an Elemental. You, though, I believe... Well, I believe you already are."

My head was beginning to spin. "Elemental?"

"Right. Able to control the elements. Like Tristan, or me." His eyes lit up as he focused again on Tristan. "Unbelievable." His eyes focused off again, and it almost looked like he was holding a silent conversation.

"Jared." Tristan voice was low and calm, and snapped Jared back. "We are not safe here. While I was being held, they injected me with drugs that I did not recognize. It's affected my memory. They also used shackles lined with osmium."

With an inward gasp, Jared stepped closer to Tristan as if to inspect him. Aden and I exchanged a helpless look but remained quiet. "Are you all right?"

"I will be. Reya has been a tremendous help. But we need to leave here."

Jared was nodding his agreement. "Of course. I can charter a jet, that way passports and whatnot won't be a problem. I have a car here; we can use it to get to the airport."

"Let's go."

We followed Jared back towards the general store and into the alley, where a rented SUV sat. Tristan and I piled into the back, letting Aden have the front.

"So, would someone please explain to me what in the world is going on?"

Jared sent me a grin through the rearview mirror. "I suppose we have a bit of time to kill on our way. I'm assuming when you say 'what's going on' you are referring to terms like 'Elemental' and 'Gifted.' Am I right?"

I crossed my arms and sent him a glare. "For starters."

He seemed a little more amused by my reaction than was healthy for him. "There are some people, obviously more than we originally thought," he looked pointedly first at me and then Aden beside him, "Who have special... gifts. A person who is fully Elemental has the ability to manipulate the elements. You know, wind, fire, water, earth. With time, we are able to shift forms. Most of us, but not all, have extra gifts."

I continued to stare at him, though my glare had reduced. He continued, "For instance, you, Reya, have a healing ability. Jace, whom you'll be meeting eventually, has the same ability. Myself, I don't have anything extra, though I suppose you could say I'm more adept at shifting than most."

"What exactly does that mean?" Aden asked through clenched teeth.

"A shifter can do exactly that- shift into another form. More than likely, it's where the legends of lycans and such came from."

Lycans. Werewolves?

"Look, no offense, but if I had any of these extra abilities, I think I would know," Aden responded.

Jared opened his mouth to speak, but Tristan beat him to it.

"You don't have these abilities yet, but you do have the potential to become like us."

Before Aden could barrage him with another round of questions, I spoke up. "Why do you think I'm already an... *Elemental*?"

Jared and Tristan shared a look in the rearview mirror. "You mean you don't know if you are?" Jared ventured to ask.

I held up my palms in exasperation. "I've never heard of any of this before today!"

Tristan ran a soothing hand down my arm, pulling me closer into his side while Jared responded.

"Reya, the way you heal people, that's not the human way. You understand that, don't you?"

"Yes," I agreed. "But all these other things, shifting and element manipulation, I can't do any of that."

"What about extremely good hearing or eyesight, fast reflexes, needing blood to survive?"

I swallowed hard as Aden's eyes met mine.

"I... I have a rare blood disease..." I stammered, not quite wanting to believe it.

Jared eyed me in the mirror. "Rare blood disease?"

"Yes, I have PKD and I have to get transfusions weekly."

"Does anyone else who has your disease get transfusions so often?" Jared asked quietly.

"No, it's more often than most but it's also an extremely rare disease, and..."

"Have you had any other complication from your disease that other people have?"

"No, I suppose not, but..." trailing off again, I became lost in a whirl of facts and figures. All the years of personal research I'd done on the topic.

"It's because you don't have PKD, Reya," Jared said softly. "And I bet you have other abilities that you've simply suppressed throughout the years in order to appear normal."

Shaking my head in denial, I looked to Tristan for help.

"This is a lot to take in, *tau o te ate*. We will get through it together."

"Give me something else to think about," I begged him. "Do you have special abilities above the normal?" I winced at my use of the word in this context.

"I am what is called a phaser." At my blank stare, he went on. "I have the ability to move through solid objects."

My eyes went wide. "Like walls?"

He nodded. "And, when the need arises, people."

Now my jaw dropped. "People?"

"Yes. It has taken a long time for that skill to develop, but I am able to overtake a person's body for a few minutes at a time."

Leaning my head back in the seat, I closed my eyes and placed a hand over my churning stomach. What in the world have I gotten myself into? Maybe when I stepped off the plane, I landed in some warped Twilight Zone episode. This was all a hoax. This had to be a hoax.

I sat back up, turning back to Tristan. "If you can phase through solid objects, why were you trapped in that tent?"

"Osmium," Tristan explained, touching his wrist in memory. "It is the densest metal on earth, and the only one I am unable to phase through."

Jared took control of the conversation again. "I know this is a lot for you both to take in. More than anything, you have my sincere gratitude for rescuing Tristan."

"The men who took my sister... are they like you?" Aden asked quietly.

"Yes," Jared answered. "But they've chosen to give up all the goodness inside themselves to become the shadow creatures. The fact that you were able to see the shadows means that you are gifted."

"What else am I able to do?" Aden wondered.

"Abilities come out differently in each person, whether they are one of the Gifted or fully Elemental. I honestly couldn't tell you."

"Tell me more about shifting. That seems like it could come in handy."

Jared grinned over at Aden. "When we first shift, we have a natural form, one that we don't have to think about to shift into. Mine is a wolf, whether because I obsessed with them as a child and so they were in my mind, or because it was passed down through my family. I'm not really sure the semantics of it."

"That's why the guard had streaks across his face. They were... they were claw marks," I murmured, staring at Tristan's hand.

Tristan smoothed a hand down my cheek. He was so gentle with me it was difficult to believe such violence could have been caused by him.

I spent the rest of the ride in silence, pondering my own thoughts, while Aden continued to speculate with Jared. Tristan's fingers lightly traced designs on the palm of my hand, and though I was still recovering from the encampment and trying to piece together all the new information, it was the most at peace I'd been.

We headed to Alice Springs, which housed a larger airport, where Jared secured a private jet for the next day. He checked us into a room and left in search of real food. While he was gone, we took turns in the shower. Other than one dip in a pond that I had talked Aden into bringing me to, it was my first shower in over two weeks. It was heaven.

When I got out, I used one of the toothbrushes Jared had asked for on check in. Since we were playing it low key, he had gotten an odd look when he asked for three brushes, since he was the only person on record in the room. But he managed to sweet-talk his way into amenities that I had sorely missed.

When I walked back into the room, Tristan was in a chair near the window and Aden was pacing the floor.

"We shouldn't have let him go on his own," Aden said.

"He had to. No one will be able to connect him to us. But if they saw him with one of us, then we'd all be in trouble," I soothed, stretching out on the bed.

He shook his head. "Still doesn't seem right."

"Jared is a fighter. He will be fine," Tristan said with absolute conviction.

Aden sank onto the opposite bed and dropped his head into his hands. "I just can't have another person hurt on my watch," he said in a low voice.

"You're not to blame, Aden. And remember my promise. We will make it right."

He said nothing, but jumped up at the three short knocks on the door. Three meant all was well; four meant trouble. Jared entered with steaming boxes of pizza and I felt my stomach flip.

"Not the healthiest of meals, but it should fill everyone up," he commented, setting down plates and drinks along with the pizza.

When he flipped open the box, I fought the urge to get up and run to the bathroom. Aden had stuck to his end of the bargain, not mentioning the baby- I really didn't want to break the news to Tristan by rushing off to puke my guts out.

"It's kind of stuffy in here, mind if I open a window?" Aden asked, taking one look at my face and understanding. I had been sick more than once in his presence in the camp.

"Sure, just keep away from view." Jared said.

I edged towards the breeze, and Tristan, and took in grateful gulps. He placed his hand on my lower back and I managed a small smile. My stomach calmed enough that I could even eat a piece of pizza without gracing everyone with its digestive reappearance.

We spent the rest of the evening carefully avoiding any paranormal conversations, and collapsed happily into bed when Jared volunteered to keep watch.

"Wake me for my turn," Aden insisted as he lay back on the bed opposite mine.

"No need," Jared told him.

I relaxed back onto the bed, laying my head against Tristan's shoulder at his insistence.

"You need your rest, too," I admonished him.

With a smirk, Jared winked at me, "We don't sleep much."

Aden popped up again. "What do you mean, you don't sleep much?"

I felt more than saw Tristan's amusement.

Jared explained, "It's one of the perks. Though, sleep does heal us, which is why Tristan needs to sleep."

"Then why have I always needed to sleep?" I ask, a small smile on my lips.

"Probably because you've been denying yourself proper nutrition," Jared muttered.

Ignore him, Reya, Tristan's voice filtered through my thoughts.

He's kind of fun to rile up, I sent back to him, unsure if I was doing it right. Earlier, when we'd had our kiss, it had seemed natural to reach out to Tristan with my mind, but now I wasn't so sure.

I have found that to be true, Tristan's amusement filled me with joy. Not only had I spoken to him, *in my mind*, but he truly seemed happy, all vestiges of his horrible ordeal forgotten, at least for the moment.

It's how I imagined it would be if I'd had a brother, I said with a note of melancholy.

Jared has become my brother, in many respects. There was a pause, then, *I did have a sister*.

Opening my eyes, I looked up and met Tristan's. He was gazing down at me, something indecipherable in his gaze.

You... did?

She was taken from me long ago, he stated this starkly, though I could see the sadness in his eyes.

I'm so sorry. I squeezed his hand once, then closed my eyes, allowing sleep to take me.

In the morning, Jared dug through his clothes and came up with outfits for the other two men. He glanced at me apologetically. "I don't have any of the female variety," he told me.

"I should hope not," I responded playfully. "Can I borrow this?" I held up a white button down that would be many sizes too large.

He shrugged. "Sure."

I changed quickly in the bathroom, wearing the same pair of jeans as before. Leaving open the last few buttons of the shirt, I tied the ends around my hips. The sleeves had to be rolled up to free my hands, but I thought all in all I pulled it off quite nicely.

We made the short trip to the airport in silence. I took in the sights as we drove. In the time I had spent here, I had slowly gotten used to the wide-open desert space. As I glanced behind me, I noted a car swerve in after us from a side street. The windows were darkly tinted, and something felt off about it.

"Jared," I started to say, but was cut short as the car put on a burst of speed and bumped us from behind. We were jolted forward, but Jared managed to stay on the road.

As he was adjusting, the car slid along beside us. All our attention was now on it, and Jared pressed the gas to outrun it, but it was too late. They jerked over and slammed into our rear, sending our car spinning donuts until we landed in a ditch.

CHAPTER 13

Even when the car stopped, my head and stomach were still spinning. Fighting nausea and reality, it seemed hours before I finally locked eyes with Tristan. He held my eyes for a brief second and then simply disappeared.

Even prepared for it, it was a shock to see a person simply disappear through solid metal. My door was yanked open and Tristan cradled me in his arms. Jared and Aden had slipped out and were huddled near us.

"Jared," Tristan said.

Jared nodded and turned to Aden. Tristan placed one hand on my cheek and left me leaning against the car.

"Take Reya and get to the airport. The pilot's name is Gary. Tell him the purple flowers are in bloom, he'll know you're with me. Wait for us for ten minutes, and if we're not back, tell him to take you to New Zealand. If we don't get to you in time, you must leave. Ten minutes," Jared waited for Aden to nod. He stood and glanced back at us. "If you do go without us, find Jace Roake. He's one of us, and he'll help you."

"No," I said. "No! We can't just leave Tristan!"

But Jared was already gone. A huge, winged shadow moved across us and Aden hauled me to my feet.

"Let's go, Reya."

"What do you mean let's go! Tristan was caught before; I can't leave him!"

Struggling against his arm, I tried to turn in the direction of the other car. I couldn't leave him, not again. He needed me.

"You're leaving me no choice," Aden warned, then swung me over his shoulder like a sack of potatoes.

At this point, I knew I was overpowered, and I really didn't want to be carried down the street like a caveman with his prize.

"Fine, Aden, put me down, I'll run."

With no argument, he set me on my feet but kept hold of my arm. We raced to the terminal and found our pilot.

I estimated Gary to be around 40, with silver streaked hair and a body that looked as if he could hold his own in a fight. A scar across his left temple told me he had. He studied us intently and I felt myself shrink back when his eyes rested on me.

"Aden Collins," Aden said, sticking his hand out. "Jared wanted me to let you know the purple flowers are in bloom."

"Good, good. I'm Gary."

"Reya," I said hesitantly, extending my hand. He took it and nodded once.

"Let's get you on board."

"We're to wait ten minutes, and Jared asked us to leave if he's not here."

Gary nodded again as he led us to the tarmac. A small, sleek plane was waiting. He gestured us up the steps and into seats.

"Get you anything before takeoff?" He asked.

I shook my head and looked helplessly out the window.

"I'll just grab us a couple waters, in case," Aden commented and left his seat. Gary sat in his place and rested a hand over mine.

"They'll be just fine, dear one. I've known Jared all my life, he can take care of things."

I nodded and felt the tears brimming. If I left Tristan here, and something happened to him- I just couldn't handle it.

The minutes ticked by until we hit ten. I was still staring out the window, willing them to appear.

"Reya," Aden began, but I stopped him.

"One more minute."

"Reya, he said ten…"

"One. More. Minute." I pronounced each word carefully in a tone that brooked no argument.

Standing, I paced to the door and watched from there. Aden joined me and stood quietly behind me. After a minute, he spoke again.

"I don't want to leave them either."

"Then don't." I snapped it out, and immediately felt bad. I knew Aden was merely doing as Jared asked.

"I'm sorry Reya, but," he paused, and I glanced back at him. "There they are!"

My head whipped around and I was down the stairs in a flash. Jared was coming through the airport doorway, his arm slung under Tristan's, supporting him. When I reached them, I took up position on his other side and took some of the weight from Jared.

"What happened to him?" I asked anxiously.

"I'm not sure, Reya. Let's get him on the plane."

Aden reached us and took over for me, and together they lifted Tristan onto the plane. Luckily, the plane had a couch that they draped Tristan across. After he was secure, they stepped back to allow me next to him.

"Let's go, Gary," Jared called up. They both took seats across from us, and I lifted Tristan's head into my lap so I could also buckle in. My hands were already streaking across his body, trying to locate the problem.

"What happened?" Aden asked this time.

"There were eight of them, four in the car that hit us and four in a car that showed up. Tristan took care of five before he went down, and I took care of the rest. I didn't see what happened, why he went down."

"Drugs," I said.

"What?" They asked simultaneously.

"They injected him with some kind of drug. I can't find it." I turned terrified eyes to them. "I know it's there, I can feel it working, but it's like the drug is made up of normal body matter and fluids. I can't trace it."

Aden and Jared exchanged a worried glance. "They were working on things like that," Aden said quietly. "I was never allowed near it. I'm sorry, I wish I knew more."

My gaze fixed on Tristan's face as I stroked his hair back. "This had to be how they captured him originally. Which means it will wear off in time, because he was very much aware when I found him, even though his memory was foggy."

They didn't answer, and I kept my eyes and thoughts on the man lying motionless in my lap.

"Come back to me," I whispered. "I need you. *We* need you."

We landed in Queenstown, where Aden and Jared loaded Tristan into the back of a four-wheel drive Jeep.

Jared drove for another two hours, until we were on the boundary of the Fiordland National Park. From there, we took dirt roads for another half an hour before following a driveway into dense trees. One minute, there was nothing but trees; the next, a huge house stood before us.

Jared stopped the car and opened his door. "Stay here," he said, and went into the trees. A few minutes later, he was back and drove us up to the house.

"What did you do?" I asked.

"There are some safeguards I had to disengage, otherwise we wouldn't have made it in."

I didn't ask for further explanation.

Entering the house, my occupied thoughts strayed enough to let out a surprised gasp. The foyer was marble and circular, with a staircase following the curve of the wall. Beyond was a great room with three-story, floor to ceiling windows. I followed the men up the stairs to the second level and saw that the landing overlooked the great room. Another set of stairs led around to the third floor, where a similar landing stood. Jared led us down a hallway and into the master suite.

We walked through a comfortable sitting room and on into the bedroom. The bed was the center of attention, carved from a dark wood with posts on each corner. They lay Tristan on it, and I sat next to him.

"Aden, I have a place not too far from here. You're welcome to stay with me for a few days," Jared said before turning to me. "We'll get some supplies for you. Is there anything that you need?"

I nodded. "He'll need to be fed intravenously. I'll make a list, if you don't mind."

"Sure thing. I'll pick up some groceries, too. There probably isn't much here."

"Thanks," I told him, and accepted the notepad he grabbed off a side table. After jotting down my list and handing it back, I looked up at him. "Could you bring back some French bread?"

"No problem," he said, and turned to leave.

"And some potato chips? And those little sour, gummy candies?"

Aden suppressed a grin while Jared nodded again. "I'll do my best."

When they reached the doorway, Jared looked back again. "For now, stay inside the house. Get some rest. I'll be back in about three hours."

Nodding, I lay down beside Tristan and fell promptly to sleep.

CHAPTER 14

A light knocking startled me out of sleep. I sat straight up and pressed a hand against my pounding heart.

Jared stood in the doorway with a few bags hanging along his arms and a box in his hands. "Hey, Reya. I'm sorry, I didn't mean to startle you."

I waved a hand in dismissal. "No, it's not you. I think I'll be waking up like that for the rest of my life."

He grinned and held out the box for me. "This is the medical equipment you asked for. Also," he gestured with the bags hanging, "in here are some clothes. A woman in town picked some stuff out. I didn't know your size, so she mostly picked out dresses and stuff. If you want, I can take you into town later so you can get more."

"I'm sure these will be fine," I told him. "Thank you."

I was surprised he had thought of it. I hadn't even considered clothes.

Taking the box, I quickly arranged the medical supplies. I set to work hooking an IV to Tristan's arm, and, satisfied everything was done, turned back to Jared.

"Come on with me," he said, walking back towards the stairs.

He led me down the wide, curving stairs and through the great room. There were French doors leading out to a small patio and the rest of the expansive property. I glanced to the right and was delighted to see a garden, overgrown as it was, with fresh vegetables and herbs. Trees were absolutely everywhere, effectively hiding the property from passerby's, by land or air.

Jared pointed out to a small group of fruit trees. "See those trees?"

"Are they guava trees?" I asked, surprised, recognizing them from our dream world.

He began walking towards them as he answered. "Yes. You'll find all kinds of edible things around here. For now, use these as a marker to how far out you can go. I can't see you needing anything else around the house, but I figured being stuck inside constantly would grate on you."

Glancing back at the house, I found myself surprised at the size of it. I must have been dazed first driving up, thinking it merely huge. It was gigantic.

"Holy cow," I breathed.

Jared smirked at me. "This is nothing. You should see my house."

My wide eyes focused on him. "Your house is bigger than this?"

"Nah," he said, the smile in his eyes. "But it's way cooler."

I shook my head, unbelieving. "What kind of fantasyland did I walk into?" I wasn't sure if I wanted him to answer or not.

I looked over to the left and spotted more large buildings. "What's in those?"

Jared looked the direction I pointed and answered, "Toys." I saw the quick grin and understood that at times, there were huge, inseparable gaps between men and women. "There's a garage, a work shed and farther back, that third building is a guest house."

My jaw dropped and my stare went back to him. "A guest house? You're kidding, right?"

He shook his head. "In one sitting you manage to swallow that I, along with Tristan, can turn into animals, and that Tristan can move through solid objects, but you're having trouble with a little guest house?"

I shrugged. "There's only so much a girl can take."

Before we went back inside, I stood on tiptoe and picked a few guavas. They would make good juice.

"Are there any other homes around here?" I asked as we started back.

"I'm the closest, about ten miles that way," he gestured towards the west, "and Jace has a residence about 15 miles that way," he gestured towards the northeast. "It's pretty secluded, since we're right on the park boundary."

"Must be lonely," I commented.

He shrugged. "It can be necessary. Trouble has a tendency to find us, and we'd rather it not intrude on innocent bystanders. We can also protect our houses better this way."

Just outside the door, he paused and seemed to gather courage. "Reya?"

Glancing up at him I answered, "Yes?"

"Does Tristan know? About the baby?"

I felt all the color drain from my face. "Did Aden tell you?" I asked, incredulous.

"No, no," he was quick to deny. "I keep up on world news. It seems you are a celebrity."

I groaned and abruptly sat down on the low step, dropping the fruit and covering my face in my hands.

Sinking down beside me, Jared put an awkward arm around my shoulder. "After you left the states, there was quite the conspiracy. No one seemed to know you went to Australia, which is also why your disappearance once you arrived went unnoticed."

My eyes met his and pleaded. "Please don't tell Tristan yet."

"Of course not. That's not my place. But I wouldn't wait too long," he gestured towards my midsection, "besides the obvious, he may also hear about it on his own." He paused again, and I could feel another question burning. I waited patiently for him to work up the courage. "Is it his?" He finally blurted out.

I nodded. "I suppose this won't sound so crazy to you, but yes, I believe so. Unless we're able to reproduce asexually?" The last I added almost hopefully.

"Sorry, no. So how...? If you don't mind me asking, that is."

I sighed, and explained the dreams. He digested the information and thought before replying.

"Tristan has had a one-track mind for the last few years. He told me he was looking for someone. I had never seen him act that way and knew it must be important. I just didn't realize..."

Trailing off, his gaze fixed out over the land. "Of course, I don't think it's crazy, but it *is* new to me. I've never heard of something like this happening before. Perhaps Dante, if I could get a hold of him, maybe Hugh..."

As he trailed off, he seemed like he was having one of those silent conversations as I had seen him have before. I decided to ask. How much stranger could all this get?

"Jared?" I asked, breaking his concentration.

He glanced at me. "Yeah?"

"You look like you're having a private conversation," I said, and raised my brows.

He stared at me for a few beats before shaking his head with a grin. "You don't miss much, do you?"

I simply kept my brows up, waiting for explanation. "My brother's name is Hugh. We're twins, and pretty closely connected. We have the ability to speak to each other."

"Telepathically?" I asked.

"Yes," he responded apprehensively.

"Okay," I said slowly, processing that information along with, apparently, my and Tristan's ability to do the same. "Are a lot of Elementals able to speak telepathically?"

Jared watched me speculatively. "In our legends, twins and mated pairs are able to speak telepathically."

I nodded, my gaze drifting towards the upstairs, where Tristan rested.

"Who's Dante?" I asked, changing the subject.

Jared looked relieved that I hadn't had a breakdown. "He's like us. He disappeared from here in the 30's and hasn't kept in contact."

"The 30's? Like the *1930's?*"

He glanced sharply at me, wary again. "Yeah."

"How do you know him?"

Jared squirmed, uncomfortable again. "Um."

Something in my memory clicked. "How old is Gary the pilot?"

Wary at my seemingly abrupt change in topic, Jared answered hesitantly, "Forty-two, I believe. Why?"

"He told me he had known you *his* entire life. And you do not look older than 42." My eyes were narrowed, my tone accusing.

"Ah, Reya," he began, and I glared more. He sighed. "It's," he gestured his hands wildly, clearly not wanting to be the one to give me this information, "one of the perks," he finally finished, defeated.

I raised an eyebrow. "Perks?"

"When we use our... abilities, we hold our youth."

"For how long?" I asked.

He shrugged. "Indefinitely."

My head spun, so I dropped it between my knees. Indefinitely? He must be joking. Taking deep breaths, I did my best to stay conscious.

"Reya? You okay?" Jared's voice was clearly on the verge of hysteria. His relief had been short lived.

With a weak nod, I managed to raise my head. "Sure. Just peachy. How are you?"

He laughed, but it held a worried edge. "Let's get you inside," he said, first bending to grab the neglected fruit and then helping me up from the step.

Opening the door, he stepped back to allow me entrance. It was cool in the house, which I was grateful for. Boston weather had done nothing to prepare me for the summer here, and with my head swirling it helped to clear the fog.

Jared led me through huge, beautifully furnished rooms until we arrived at the kitchen. Bags lined the counters and he immediately began unpacking.

"I just got some basics," he said, understanding the precarious edge I was on and attempting to keep the subject light.

My eyebrows rose again as I took in the amount of food in front of me. "Basics? It looks like you could feed an army for a week," I commented.

He grinned and brought an armful to the fridge. I took a minute to look around and was completely awed. With the amount of time I spent working, I had never seriously considered owning or decorating a house. Now, seeing this one, I realized it was exactly how I would want one, should I ever get around to it.

Every room I had seen so far was light and open, with floor to ceiling windows more often than not. The floors were either dark wood or white marble and gorgeous. Off the impressively modern kitchen was a large dining room with floor to ceiling windows on three sides, with a view of the deep forest beyond.

"So, why *did* you come to Australia?" Jared asked.

I glanced at him, surprised. My original intention had been forgotten with everything else. "Oh," I said, rubbing my temple. "My parents, before they died, left me an inheritance. I never touched it, so it's been sitting in an account in Ayers Rock. I thought, or was hoping, that it might lead me to clues about me."

I realized that, in a big way, it had.

"You never knew your parents?" Jared asked, his eyebrows knitting together.

"No. I was very young when they died, and I grew up in a state-run home."

"Hmm," he said, and grabbed an armful for the cabinet. "And you never got a chance to go, did you?"

I shook my head. "No," I told him. Most of my questions had been answered, but now I was curious to what I would find.

Rubbing a hand across his jaw, Jared thought for a moment before returning to his task. He finished unloading and handed me a tiny black phone. "This is a secure number," he explained. "You can use it to contact me, or call back to the States if you need to."

"Thank you," I said sincerely. Isabel came to mind and I immediately felt the guilt. She must be worried sick.

"There's something else," Jared hesitated, seeming concerned that I was going to have a break down.

"Go ahead, Jared. Let's tear off all the Band-Aids."

His quick grin showed his relief. "Tristan will need more than an IV to heal properly," he began, walking to the wall just outside the kitchen. "As will you."

With bated breath I watched as he placed his palms in two different locations and uttered a word in an unfamiliar language. The wall began to slide open, revealing a small room between the back of the kitchen appliances and the next room.

"What is this?" I breathed, stepping in with Jared.

"One of the emergency arsenals," Jared answered me.

I took in the various weapons lining the walls and realized this just may be my tipping point.

"Why would I need any of this?" I asked, my voice still barely above a whisper.

"You shouldn't," Jared told me. "But you will need this."

Pulling open a small refrigerator unit, he carefully took out several bags and handed them to me.

Blood bags.

"You're kidding," I stared at the bags.

"Unfortunately, no."

"And, I'm guessing, you don't expect me to intake these with a needle."

"I realize you're still uncomfortable with the idea of taking the nutrients orally," Jared said, "so if you'd prefer to do the transfusion as you're used to, that's fine."

I took a breath before responding. "I think for now, it would be best."

He grinned at me again. "I understand. Let me show you how to open this yourself, in case you need to. Otherwise, let's keep a few bags in the main fridge."

Nodding, I took the bags in my hands and left them in the kitchen before returning to the wall.

"Place your hands here, and here," Jared guided me. "Feel the small indent on this side, and the bump on this side?"

"Yes," I answered him.

"Okay, repeat after me. *Tuwhera.*"

The word felt funny on my lips, but I repeated it as best I could. To my surprise, and delight, the wall slid back open.

"To close, put your hands in the same spot, and say *Kati.*"

I did, then practiced a few more times until Jared was satisfied I could do it on my own before walking back to the kitchen.

"Anything else you need before I go?" He asked, studying my features.

I shook my head. "I don't think so."

As he started towards the door, I stopped him. "Jared?"

"Yeah?" He asked, glancing over his shoulder.

"Those other men, the ones at the camp- we'll get them out, won't we?"

His eyes narrowed. "*We* won't, no. You'll stay here, safe. But yes, I will be going back, with Aden and hopefully Tristan."

I opened my mouth to argue but shut it again, nodding instead. We'd see about that.

Once he left, I grabbed the bag of potato chips Jared had graciously brought and ripped it open. My diet of rice and mushy surprise had left me with unbearable cravings. I walked to the window and gazed out, crunching down on a chip. It was salty and perfect. The trees were so beautiful here, I thought with a sigh. So much like the dream place I had imagined so many times. Just then I remembered something Tristan had told me in a dream. *But I live here*, he had said. My heart banged out one heavy beat and returned to normal. It shouldn't surprise me, not now. Somehow, we had connected and that's all there was to it.

I fixed a cheese sandwich and picked up two of the blood bags, carrying it all upstairs to look over Tristan. Though I had no idea how long he would be unconscious, I was determined he would not wake alone.

The sun was setting as I examined him, preparing to set up a blood transfusion. An idea came to me, and I slipped a needle from the supplies Jared had brought me. If this maniacal group was larger than the one that had held us, and by my suspicions it was, then this drug could be used against more people in the future. Jared had mentioned another healer, and perhaps between the two of us we could discover what the drug consisted of.

Carefully, I drew a vial of blood from Tristan's arm and stored it for study later before setting up the blood bag. That done, I sighed, smoothing a hand across his forehead and rising, stretching my back, realizing how sore I was. I made my way to the bathroom that was larger than my entire apartment back home and spent time in the shower, attempting to ease the tension in my muscles. Showering was definitely a luxury I had always taken for granted.

Stepping out of the shower, I found a large, fluffy white robe and slipped it on. The windows here overlooked the back of the house, and I could see the roofs of the outbuildings. Including, I thought with a shudder, the guesthouse.

Digging through the bags Jared had left, I found drawstring pants and a spaghetti strap shirt. They were still a little large, but I knew that would change in a few weeks.

Glancing at the clock, I picked up the small black phone Jared had left me. I did the mental math and realized it would be too early to call Boston. Another hour, and I just might be forgiven.

As the phone rang, I thought through what I would say. When her voicemail picked up, I took a deep breath before speaking. "Isy, it's Reya. I don't have much time, I just wanted you to know I'm all right. I promise to call you soon and explain the best I can. I love you."

CHAPTER 15

"Focus, Reya. Try again."

I stared down at the pile of dirt with annoyance. Sitting on the ground with the hot sun shining on my back left me in no mood for niceties.

"This is ridiculous," I huffed, crossing my arms across my chest. Jared expected me to focus on the earth, and get it to move. With my mind. What a nut.

"Just one more time. And then I promise, we can go back in."

For the last two hours, he had been teaching me how to tap into my abilities to control the elements. So far, the closest I came to moving the earth was when I felt an overwhelming urge to throw the dirt in his face.

Jared sat comfortably across from me in a small spot of grass in the large yard. Letting out an exasperated breath, I focused on the ground. Clearing my mind, I waited for something to happen. Anything.

After a minute I shook my head. "This isn't working."

"All right, let's call it quits for today. You don't want to push it too hard," Jared said, a slight scowl on his face. I wasn't sure if he was frustrated with me, or himself.

Gratefully, I stood and returned to the cool interior. Grabbing a bottle of water, I hurried up the stairs and into the bedroom, where Aden was watching over Tristan.

Aden, perched in a chair near the window, grinned up at me from over a book he had been reading. "Fun, isn't it?"

I rolled my eyes and ran my hands over Tristan. It had been two days and no change as yet. "A blast. Nothing?"

He shook his head. "It can't be much longer, though."

Pressing my lips together, I nodded. "How is your practice going?"

"Jared told me not to expect much, since I'm not fully Elemental, but," He shrugged, a satisfied smile on his face, "I lifted fruit off the ground."

"You did?" I asked, surprised.

Jared entered the room and lounged on a small couch that sat in front of a fireplace. Part of me wished it were cool enough to light a fire, as inviting as the space around it was. It was all too easy to imagine curling up with a good book, the blazing fire the only light.

"He did," Jared confirmed. "He seems to have a knack for wind."

That was seriously cool. I turned my attention to Jared and asked the burning question. "Have you guys decided when to leave?"

Jared shook his head. "Hugh is caught up at the moment, as is Jace. I'd really like at least three of us before we attempt anything."

I nodded, worrying my lower lip. I'd rather they didn't have to go at all. But involving the local police was out of the question. What would we say?

A maniacal group is torturing men they believe have supernatural powers. How do you know this? *Well, you see, I was being held prisoner because I have special healing powers. Aden here was the one who kidnapped me, and Tristan- who I met in my dreams- was being held captive.*

Right. We'd be locked up instead.

So, instead, I waited out the days, practicing with Jared and reading to Tristan. I also slept. A lot.

Though the house- well, technically, the mansion- was huge, I rarely left the room that held Tristan. I read from the books that he had on a shelf, even when Jared assured me there was a library where I could find a much wider selection. I didn't say this aloud, but I figured Tristan would only keep books he was especially fond of so close to him, and was hoping between my voice and the words on the page that it would help bring him back sooner. The only other room I was familiar with was the kitchen, where I made meals and hurried back upstairs.

I called Isy again the second night, knowing I had to come up with some kind of story. What could I say? *Hey Isy, remember when I muttered 'Tristan' in my sleep? Well, it turns out I was taking spirit trips to New Zealand and managed to get myself knocked up.*

I winced at the phrase that had popped into my head as the phone rang at my ear.

"Isy, it's Reya," I said when she picked up.

"Thank goodness! How are you? Do you have time to talk?"

"As much as you need," I assured her.

"All right, start explaining."

Taking a deep breath, I began telling her a story I'd rehearsed in my head. "The truth is, my parents set me up with an arranged marriage before I was born. He's been to visit me a few times, and we've stayed in contact in between. The last time he was there, we... got intimate."

"I can't believe you didn't tell me this!" Isy seemed outraged about being left in the dark. After she calmed down, she asked, "Are you happy with him?"

Glancing at his prone form lying on the bed, I answered her, "Yes."

She gave an audible sigh. "I don't forgive you yet, but tell me all about him. What's his name, where's he from, where are you?"

Laughing, I did my best to appease her. "His name is Tristan. He's from New Zealand, as were my parents. It's a very close knit community here, and I've met some pretty amazing people. I'm staying with him right now, he lives on the border of a national park. It's beautiful."

"It all sounds very romantic, but you had me and Ben worried sick. Don't ever do that again."

"I'll do my best. We'll come visit as soon as we're able, and you'll get to meet him for yourself. Then you'll see I'm in good hands. Isy," I hesitated, knowing I had to be careful what I said here. "You know me better than anyone. You're the only one who really knew about my... special ability. The thing is, Tristan is like me."

"He can heal people too?" She asked, confused.

"No, but he can do... other things."

There was a long silence where I wasn't sure she was going to respond.

"There's obviously more to the story you're not telling me, and I understand that you won't want to speak over the phone. I expect you to tell me everything when I see you in person."

"I promise," I told her.

"What do you want me to tell Ben? I mean, you told him you were a virgin. He's very confused, and he'll think that you lied to him."

Sighing, I closed my eyes, thinking through my options. "Tell him what I told you, except about his special abilities. When I see him next, I'll smooth things over. And... tell him I'm sorry. That goes for you, too. I'm sorry for worrying you."

"We worry because we care. Take care of yourself, mama," she said, and I could almost see her smile at the words.

"You got it."

The night of the third day, I sat in a chair pulled up beside the bed and read from The Call of the Wild. Just as I was getting through Buck's first night in the strange camp, a low sound had my eyes flicking up. Tristan's eyes were watching me, dark and glittering in the low light.

With a gasp I stood beside the bed and ran my hands over him. "Tristan! How do you feel? Are you okay?

In response, his hands framed my face, his thumbs running along my jaw. "No, no," I reprimanded him, eyeing the IV. Gently, I took his hands and positioned them on his sides. "Let me get the IV out before you try that."

He watched me without blinking, which normally would have been unnerving if it weren't for the utter relief and joy I felt rushing through me. Deftly I freed him from the wires and tubes before helping him sit up.

"How do you feel?" I asked again, searching his face.

"I'm fine." His words were low and husky.

"Let me get you some tea," I said, jumping up. He wrapped his hand easily around my wrist, effectively holding me in place.

"No," he said. "Stay."

It was illogical, but I obediently sat again. The look on his face was so fragile I didn't dare disobey.

"Do you remember what happened?" I asked softly, worried for a bad reaction.

He shook his head slightly, his eyes still boring into mine. "Not clearly. It will come back."

I nodded, still watching him anxiously. This drug was out of my realm, so I tread lightly. We sat like that, quiet and motionless, for a long time. I felt all the tension of the last few days drain out of me with the simple pleasure of looking at him, awake and alert.

Finally, I shook myself out of the moment and smiled. "Let me get you something to eat. It's been so long since you've had solid food. And some tea would help your throat." He started to object, but I placed a hand on his cheek. "I'll be right back, just a few minutes. Let me do this for you."

He nodded, his eyes on mine until I was out of sight. Running to the kitchen, I put some bread in the toaster and heated a kettle of water for tea. As I was buttering the toast, the kettle whistled. I put in a combination of elm bark and mullein, topping it off with some honey to help soothe the throat and brought it all upstairs on a tray.

When I entered the room, Tristan was standing, leaning heavily against the bed. I gasped, practically throwing the tray onto a table and rushing to his side.

"What are you doing?" I wrapped my arms around him in an attempt to force him back on the bed.

He didn't answer, but allowed me to help him back down. I shoved the pillows behind his back for comfort and retrieved the tray.

"I don't want you getting up until I'm here to help you. Now drink this, and I have some toast for you. If there's no problems, then I'll make you something more to eat."

He took the cup, his eyes still on me. He reminded me so much of an animal it was frightening.

After he ate the toast and drank two cups of tea, he spoke. "Where are Jared and Aden?"

"They're at Jared's house. They've been over every day, helping me out."

He nodded. "How long have we been back here?"

"Three days. How's the memory?" I smoothed back his hair before setting aside the tray.

"I remember escaping, and meeting Jared again. After that, it's a little hazy." His eyes lowered and I knew he was frustrated.

"You have a beautiful house here," I said, hoping to distract him. It worked. Flicking his gaze back to me, the edges of a smile played at his lips.

"You like it?"

I nodded. "Very much. I haven't seen all of it, but the kitchen and this room are great." I let out a short laugh that had Tristan's mouth turning down.

"Why haven't you seen anything but the kitchen and here?"

My grin stayed in place. "Silly. I've been here, with you."

This brought back the smile, in full force. It lifted my spirits to see it.

"That means I can give you a tour," he said.

"Sounds good to me. Just not tonight. I want you to rest a bit more."

"Yes, doctor," he said playfully. "You are a doctor now, aren't you?"

The statement gave me pause. It was startling to realize how little we really knew of each other. "Yes, I am. I received my license last summer."

"Congratulations," he said, pinching a section of hair between his fingers and tugging lightly. "We'll have to celebrate."

"Really," I said, "and how would we celebrate?"

"Any way you want. How about a trip?"

I laughed bitterly. "The last trip didn't work out so well." His smile faltered and I was instantly regretful. "Except that it brought me to you," I amended.

This seemed to mollify him, but there was worry in his eyes. "What would you like then?"

"Hmm," I said, tapping my finger against my chin, "Do you cook?"

This seemed to take him aback. "Cook?" He repeated, as if the word was foreign.

"Yes. Bake, grill, toss? Any of the above?"

He was hesitant in answering. "Yes, of course."

My smile spread across my face. "Great. When you're all better, you can cook for me to celebrate."

"It's a deal." One of his thumbs brushed just beneath my eye. "You look tired," he said softly.

"Hardly. I've slept more in the last three days than I have in the last three years combined."

That statement didn't help much. "Someone needs to take care of you," he said, his brows knitted and his tone serious. I laughed again at his utter ridiculousness.

"I've done pretty well on my own." But his expression didn't change, and I sighed. "All right. If I rest, you will too."

In response, he tugged my hand until I lay beside him. I moved the pillows from behind him so he could lay back. He locked my hand between his chest and both of his hands, and I fell easily into sleep.

In the morning, my eyes slid open and for the first time in weeks, I felt refreshed. As I blinked the object in front of me into focus, I realized it was Tristan's face, and his eyes were on me.

"Good morning," he whispered gently.

My eyes lit with happiness. He was real, and he was alive. "Good morning."

"You look so peaceful in sleep," he murmured. His face was close to mine, as was his body, and I could feel a response throughout all my limbs.

"You haven't been watching me this whole time, have you?" My eyes darted to the windows to see the bright stream of sun shining through. Judging by the angle of the rays, it must be just past dawn.

"Not long. I *have* been sleeping for three days, you know," Tristan teased.

Everything in me wanted to prolong the moment, but the doctor in me was overpowering.

"I'll make you something to eat," I said, sitting up and stretching.

"There's something else I would like," Tristan said, and sat up too.

I glanced at him. "Anything."

"A shower."

Grinning in understanding, I stood and helped him up. "Just take it slow, please. I don't think you were fully healed from the last round of this stuff."

He shrugged. "I'm a fast healer."

"Of course," I said sarcastically. Though, from what Jared told me, Elementals had abnormally good immune systems- I supposed that explained why I'd never been sick a day in my life. The drugs that Donovan's men were developing were a bit different than the common cold, however.

We reached the bathroom and I was faced with a dilemma. The shower was one of those big, wide-open deals with multiple shower heads. And although Tristan and I had been…intimate, that was in a dream. And this was real life.

He seemed to read my expression and smiled gently. "Just help me inside," he said.

Obliging, I walked with him until he was propped against the wall. When I turned to leave, he pulled on my hand again. "Give me a second," he said, and sounded out of breath.

Turning back, I let out a screech when a stream of cool water hit my head. I stared up at him in disbelief, but his grin was unrepentant. "There," he said smugly, "Now you can stay."

I was still staring in wide-eyed shock as his hands grasped under my jaw and lifted my face to his. His mouth came down on mine, soft and sweet. Without thought, my entire body reacted, again. Forgetting that he needed to take it easy, my hands snaked around his neck and I clung to him, silencing the tiny voice inside that was trying to reprimand. In quick moves our clothes were gone and his hands easily lifted me, my legs wrapping around his waist.

Reya, his voice whispered across my mind. *You need to feed.*

My thoughts were in a haze of warmth, love, and, most welcome, lust. *Tristan*. His name was a safe haven in the storm of emotion pouring through me.

Take what you need, tau o te ate. Images flitted through my mind's eye, an overpowering need to take what was being offered.

My mouth nuzzled into his throat, and, as if it were the most natural thing in the world, I felt my incisors lengthen into points. Gently pressing them into his skin, I felt the first burst of energy, sheer power rushing into my system.

I took his very essence into my body as he took me, the water cascading down around us in sheets.

As our bodies shuddered with release, I pulled my head back, my eyes large and dazed.

"Tristan," my voice was low, filled with awe. "I… I had no idea."

"Neither did I, *tau o te ate*."

"You mean taking blood isn't always like that?"

Tristan laughed, carefully setting me on my feet. "No, Reya, and thank God it's not. Though, just in case, perhaps you should never feed from anyone else."

I let out a shaky laugh. "That's fine by me."

He brushed a thumb across my cheek, just under my eye. "I had heard stories of what it is like for mates. They didn't do it justice."

When Jared and Aden arrived later that morning, I was at the stove cooking up breakfast with Tristan at the table, watching me carefully. Although his strength had obviously returned, I smiled to myself at the thought, I still wanted him to take it easy. He insisted on going downstairs with me, and unwillingly accepted my terms to sit and do nothing else.

"Mm," Jared said appreciatively. "Smells good."

He leaned over my shoulder to take in a whiff of the eggs and bacon I had frying side by side. I laughed and shooed him away.

"Sit down like a good boy, and you'll get some. Morning, Aden," I added with a grin over my shoulder.

He eyed me critically but seemed to accept my good mood as a result of Tristan's recovery. "Morning," he returned the greeting before slipping into a chair across from Tristan. "Good to see you up and about," he said to Tristan.

"Thank you," Tristan answered, though I could still feel his eyes on me.

Jared sat too, eager to please me for his reward. "When did you come around?" He asked Tristan, and I heard him bite into an apple.

"Last night. I am feeling no ill effects today, so I will be ready to go with you."

I spun around, surprised. I hadn't told him about the planned return trip, and this was the first time he had seen Jared or Aden. Aden's expression mirrored my own, but Jared was nodding.

"We'll leave tomorrow."

Tristan's gaze had strayed to Jared but was immediately back on mine. At the look on my face, he began to rise, but I stopped him.

"You sit back down," I reprimanded. "How did you know they were going?"

Tristan sat again, clearly torn. "It is what I would do," he answered in a calm voice.

"Oh," I said, and turned back to the breakfast. Quickly I dished it out and went to sit with the three men.

Jared and Aden dug in with gusto, obviously not used to being cooked for. Tristan grasped my hand and held it while we all ate in silence. I was the first to break it.

"I want to come with."

The denial was instant and unanimous. Patiently I waited for them to calm, and spoke again.

"I don't want to help you, exactly," I said slowly, wanting to make my point. "But the men that are in the camp need medical assistance. It would be better for me to be near, to help them."

The denials were still there, but had lost some steam. "Also," I continued, unhampered, "I would like to visit the lawyer in Ayers Rock. The whole reason I flew here, in the first place."

It was silent for a moment, until Tristan spoke quietly. "We can go there anytime you wish."

With a gentle squeeze on the hand surrounding mine, I answered, "Thank you. But why not now? I'm assuming you plan on entering the camp at night," I paused, and the silence was my answer. "So we can fly in tomorrow afternoon. The three of you can come with me, my big strong protectors, and I'll wait a safe distance away, or even on the plane, for you to come back."

Jared and Aden exchanged a glance, clearly worried but swayed by my logic. Tristan, of course, kept his eyes on me.

"She has a point," Jared said quietly. There was a low, grumbling sound emanating from Tristan's throat, but Jared persisted. "Jace can't make it, not so soon. If he could, then I would say absolutely not. But if she stays on the plane," he trailed off, and waited for Tristan to meet his gaze.

"On the plane," he said intensely, his eyes boring into mine.

"I promise," I told him solemnly.

"Is there anything I can say to talk you out of it?"

I shook my head. "Probably not."

His eyes stayed hard but he nodded and directed his attention to Jared. "Fine. Set it up."

"I was also wondering if you could try to get a hold of the drug they're using," I told them.

Jared was already nodding. "That was part of the plan. Rescuing the captives takes precedence, of course, but if we could get our hands on at least some of their research, it would give us a leg up."

"You must do something for me today," Tristan said, his sole focus on me.

I raised a brow. "What is that?"

"I'd like you to practice again, using the elements."

I glanced briefly at Jared. "That hasn't been going too well."

"This time you'll have me. I will guide you."

Nodding, I agreed.

"Plus, now that you've taken blood properly, I think you'll be surprised at how much more power you have," Jared added.

My eyes widened as I turned to him. "How do you know that?"

Jared looked from me to Tristan and back again, realizing he may have overstepped his bounds. "I can tell."

Feeling my cheeks redden, I stood to clear the plates. Aden was clearly lost, but he spoke up. "I'll see to the dishes, you go and practice," he told me.

Not making eye contact with either Aden or Jared, I walked over to Tristan, wrapping an arm around his waist. It did seem his strength had completely returned, but I *was* still a doctor.

We walked outside and settled on the ground. Tristan arranged me in front of him so I could lean back into his chest, his arms wrapped around my waist. His mouth was at my ear as he spoke in low, velvet tones.

"Close your eyes. Imagine what you want to have happen there first, then open your eyes and think of only that."

My eyes closed, I did just that. We were surrounded by grass, and I concentrated hard. Though I'd always been better with facts and numbers, I reminded myself that I had imagined a secret place where I'd met Tristan, and I could do this.

"Build the image in your mind's eye, and keep it as the top layer of images when you open your eyes," Tristan's voice enveloped me in its warmth.

Finally, I slid my eyes open, doing as he said. My imaginative scene interfaced with reality, transposing itself. The earth began to move, just slightly at first, a low rumbling, before bursting forth into the shape of a small hill at my feet.

I frowned at it, unimpressed.

"What is it, *tau o te ate*?"

"That's supposed to be a sandcastle," I grumbled.

I could feel his lips curve against my neck. "It's a start."

CHAPTER 16

With a vague feeling of chagrin, I stared down at the unbuttoned fly of the pants I was trying on. Apparently, over the last few days, I had gained a few extra pounds. It was difficult to notice, with the loose dresses and pajama bottoms that my wardrobe consisted of nowadays.

I stuck my head out and smiled shyly at the helpful clerk. "Could I have the next size up?" I asked her.

When Tristan had agreed to letting me accompany them back to Ayers Rock, I realized I really didn't have an outfit for the trip. Sure, a sundress would be fine for the appointment I had with the lawyer, but an uneasy feeling plagued me about the trip, so I wanted to be ready for anything.

All three men had come with me to town, but only Aden had escorted me into the store, leaving Jared and Tristan to make last minute arrangements and plans. I grabbed my items and hurried out of the dressing room.

"Thanks for doing this," I said to Aden. "I know this can't be fun for you."

He shrugged. "At least it's a change of pace. Can't remember the last time I was in a store like this."

I laughed at his expression and answered him companionably. "Me either. Even back in Boston, I wasn't exactly a girly girl."

He shuddered. "Thank goodness."

I hauled my selections to the check out. He eyed them suspiciously.

"What's with the ninja outfit?"

I blushed but turned my attention to the clerk. For the meeting, I had gotten a white pantsuit with a nice red shirt to go beneath it. Red always made me feel a little more confident. The other items I got were black, stretchy pants and a black, long sleeved shirt. It figures this wouldn't slip past Aden's inquiring gaze.

I didn't answer until we were leaving. "It's an outfit to change into afterwards," I explained. "All I have are dresses, and I didn't think a white pantsuit would do, with the condition those men will be in."

The explanation was good, solid, and I hoped he bought it completely. It was a reason- just not the only reason.

It seemed to placate him, and we wandered a bit in town before meeting Jared and Tristan near the airport.

"Can I say something, if you promise not to get freaked out?" Aden's voice was hesitant and I glanced at him.

"Sure, Aden," I told him. What now?

"It's just that- well, I'm glad to see you happy." He hesitated before finishing, as if changing his thought halfway through.

"Okay," I said slowly. "Thank you?" It came out more as a question than a sentiment.

He laughed, his cheeks flushing. "That's not exactly what I meant," he said and I waited. "Not that I'm not glad to see you happy, I am." He stopped abruptly, and I had to spin on my heel to face him. His eyes were averted from mine. "I feel this really odd connection to you. Not like the connection you and Tristan have," he continued in a rush, "But it's something. Almost like I feel about Aurelia."

My heart went out to him when his voice broke on his sister's name. "Aden, don't be embarrassed. Remember Jared explained that to us, sort of?" It had been on the second day Tristan was unconscious. Jared attempted to explain the connection Elementals had to one another. It made sense; the reason Aden felt so compelled to stay by me, and the pull he felt from Tristan, too. Why he risked getting in trouble to have me heal him.

He was shaking his head. "It's more than that. I feel the pull to them, but it's like I feel it more with you. Ten times more. It's a little disconcerting."

"Hmm," I murmured, and began walking again. "You know, I think I do know what you mean. It's like when I got into the taxi with you," he slumped his shoulders, so I laughed. "Don't feel bad about that, Aden. You brought me to Tristan, so in the end, it worked out okay."

"Tell that to my conscious," he grumbled.

"One day you'll believe it," I said firmly. "Anyway, I wouldn't have gotten in the taxi with you if I hadn't felt some pull. It's like I was immediately comfortable in your presence. And then when Jared showed up, I knew right away that he wasn't bad, but there was still hesitation on my part."

"That could be because you just escaped a camp full of fanatics," Aden interrupted me.

"True," I pursed my lips. "But I don't think so. Did I tell you Jared thinks we're related?"

This snapped his head up. "Really?"

"Yeah. He says it's the hair," I laughed. "But also my last name, Tane. It's a local name, and was in his family centuries ago. We'd be cousins or something. That whole immortality thing kind of freaks me out."

I admitted the last sheepishly. Aden nodded. "Me too. Although, it does give me hope." At my inquiring glance, he continued. "Jared said how resilient we are. We can be killed, but it isn't easy. Even me, though I'm not fully Elemental. Which explains the heart attack," he paused and rubbed his chest, just as he had the first time he told me about it. "Jared said that would have killed anyone else."

My eyes narrowed. I hadn't known that. A flash of memory threatened, but I dismissed it. Then the pieces came together. "So it gives you hope for your sister," I said quietly.

He nodded. "I won't stop searching until I find out what happened to her. One way or another."

Instinctively, I grabbed his hand and gave it a gentle squeeze. He smiled and our eyes met in complete understanding.

The flight was tense. Jared was worried about the lawyer. If my parents were, in fact, Elementals, it would make sense for them to use someone trustworthy. He was worried because he had never heard of Malakai Scott.

I was nervous, too. Somehow, I had managed my whole life without giving my origins much thought. Now, for better or worse, I would learn more about the people who brought me into the world.

But that was merely the tip of the iceberg. My stomach was in knots at the thought of Tristan going back to that awful place. I wasn't sure if I could stand anything else happening to him. Even in the short time I had known them, I also felt fiercely protective of Jared and Aden. They were quickly becoming the family I had never had. Glancing over at Jared and his red-streaked hair, I amended that thought. He might not just be *like* family, he might *be* family.

At the airport, a car was waiting for us. Jared took the wheel and drove directly to the small office that held the law practice of Scott and Scott. When I'd done some research on Malakai Scott, I'd found out he and his brother ran the practice together, but there wasn't much more to be found online.

Jared and Aden had decided to stay outside and watch for trouble, while Tristan accompanied me inside.

Tristan paused in the doorway and looked me up and down. "You look beautiful," he said, and my heart flipped. I had changed into the new outfit on the plane, and managed my unruly hair into the wretched bun. "But you seem to be missing something," he said thoughtfully.

I glanced down, wondering if I had forgotten shoes or a button on my shirt. When I looked back up, Tristan was examining something in his hand.

"These will go nicely," he murmured before meeting my gaze. "Would you do me the honor of wearing them?"

I studied his hand again, more intently. There were two teardrop shaped stones, a beautiful amber color. They were held by a gold clasp with a diamond winking in the fading light.

I gasped, "Tristan," but he cut me off.

"It would please me very much to see you wear them," he said and gently slid them into my ears. Ridiculously, I felt tears brimming in my eyes. Must be the mood swings.

"Thank you," I said with a clogged throat.

"Perfect," he appraised. "They match your eyes beautifully."

He turned and opened the door for me to enter.

The receptionist greeted us warmly. It was merely seconds before an older, dark-skinned man with kind eyes came out to meet us.

"Ms. Tane, so very nice to meet you." He shook my hand, clasping it in both of his. His attention turned to Tristan and he held a surprised look in check. "Mr. Amiri."

A look of shock crossed my own face, and Tristan looked confused as well. My shock was two-fold; not only that this stranger seemed to know Tristan, but also that I hadn't even known his last name. At least, I didn't remember ever asking it. Oh, no. I was about to have a baby with someone and I didn't even know his last name!

I felt a gentle squeeze on my hand and attempted to control my breathing. Our sudden silent wariness didn't seem to faze Mr. Scott, and he swiftly led us back to his office.

"Forgive me," he said, an edge of excitement apparent in his voice. "I just never thought," he trailed off and let out an unexpected squeal of excitement. I exchanged a helpless glance with Tristan, who seemed as lost as I was.

"Please, please sit," he gestured towards the chairs in front of a desk.

We sat, and I kept Tristan's hand in a death grip. All the nerves had spilled over and my emotions were haywire. He seemed to instinctively know this, and remained perfectly calm.

"Mr. Scott," he said, his voice quiet authority. "Forgive our apprehension, but you seem to know more of us than we do of you."

"Oh yes, yes, I realize how this must seem to you." His eyes shot to me and seemed to gleam from the inside out. "You look so much like her."

My heart skipped a beat and I managed a whisper. "Like who?"

"Your mother, of course," his eyes softened and his voice turned wistful. "She was beautiful. I was young, and a stammering idiot around her, I'm afraid."

He chuckled then, in remembrance of some personal joke. "But your father," he shook his head now, but the light still remained. "I wasn't stupid enough to mess with him."

Clearing my unexpectedly clogged throat, I asked, "You knew them?"

"Oh, yes. I'm so sorry; I realize you were very young when they died. You see, my family has known about magic for generations, and is sworn to protect the secret."

In the stunned silence, Mr. Scott merely smiled. "In the western world, such things seem fanciful, don't they? But you, Ms. Tane, are from a great lineage that holds immense power. As are you, Mr. Amiri."

There it was again, the reverence when he spoke Tristan's name. My confusion only grew.

"Please, call me Tristan. May I ask how you know me, Mr. Scott?"

"And please, call me Malakai. Are you familiar with our dreamtime?"

Tristan nodded once, and I held silent. We only had a certain amount of time, so I would have Tristan explain things to me later.

"Much of our culture has been lost over the centuries. *Karadji*, or Medicine Men, have almost become extinct. Not many believe in the old ways anymore," he shrugged as if this didn't bother him. "Even we need to stay with the times. But my family, passed down from son to son, is one of the few that still follows the old practices. My father, and my father's father, and so on, have gone through the rituals to become *Karadji*. For some reason, the magic runs strong in us. Others go through the same rituals, but my family has the visions."

I wished I had spent more time on this culture. So far, not much of what he said made sense, but Tristan seemed entranced.

"I didn't realize there was still a line so powerful," he commented.

Malakai smiled then. "Yes. My own son is going through the process right now."

"Congratulations. You must be proud."

"Of course, of course. So, you see, in our visions, we have seen the spirit of your ancestors and have known that our line would, at some time or another, help yours. Truth be told, I didn't expect it to happen in this lifetime."

Tristan was quiet for a moment before he spoke. "How did you come across Reya's parents?"

Malakai's eyes went dreamy again, wistful. "She came to me in a vision. Beautiful, a goddess. She was powerful, more powerful than any I've come across in all my years."

"What could she do?" I asked hesitantly.

"She could connect her spirit to others. People can be difficult to read, but your spirit cannot hide its true way. We believe, correctly," he winked, "that when a person sleeps, their spirit drifts. Your mother was so in tune with her own spirit, that she could find others. She found me."

"Why?" My curiosity overcame any anxiety.

"To help you, of course."

Tristan interrupted this time. "Was she a foreseer?"

Malakai shook his head. "No. Her husband was."

Tristan sucked in an audible breath, but I wasn't sure why. How could any of this surprise him, of all people?

"A male?" He asked, a mixture of hope and skepticism clear in his voice.

"That's right. Amazing, the two of them were. He had foreseen their death, and knew there was no way to prevent it. And the course of Reya's life had a very exact line that it needed to follow."

Confusion overwhelmed me again. "What course?"

"Why, the one leading you to Tristan."

I glanced at him and felt my stomach twist. My parents- my father- had foreseen Tristan?

"I was not to contact you until your eighteenth birthday. This set in motion a course of events which led you to here."

I paled and felt my head spin. This was getting to be a little too much.

"Reya?" Tristan's anxious voice was close, and I realized he had crouched before me. My blurry gaze fixed on him, but it didn't halt the spinning.

I heard the door open, and a few minutes later a glass of water was shoved to my mouth. Taking a sip, I sank my head between my knees.

"I'm sorry," I mumbled, not sure if they could hear me. I felt soothing hands on my back and struggled to get a grip. Slowly, I raised my head and managed a small smile at Tristan. "Overload."

He smiled back, but worry was etched into his face. *We can leave now, if you wish.*

No, I sent back to him. *I want to know. I need to know.*

I glanced at Malakai, standing uncomfortably near my chair. It was probably the first time someone had come close to passing out in his office.

"I'm okay," I promised them both, and took another sip of water.

"Perhaps we'll save stories for another time. You wish to see what has been left for you."

This last was a statement, not a question, but I nodded anyway. He stood and held open his door.

"Please, come with me. The bank is directly across the street, that is where the box has been held for you."

We followed him into another small building, directly across from his office, as promised. The teller acknowledged him with a smile and, after having me sign the appropriate paperwork, led us to a back hallway. Malakai must have arranged this ahead of time.

After leaving us in a tiny room with a table and a few chairs, the teller promised she'd be back quickly. I sat staring at the wall with Tristan next to me, one arm slung across my shoulders. He always seemed to be touching me in some way, needing the contact. Not that I minded it- it was nice to know he was real. Perhaps a little disconcerting, though. Growing up I had never had close friends, and even Isabel seemed to understand my need for personal space.

At the thought of my best friend, my stomach gave a little twist. Isabel. I still wasn't sure what to do about her, or Ben, or Boston in general.

Tristan felt my sudden tension and tightened his hold on my shoulders. It didn't do much to relieve my anxiety.

The helpful teller reentered the room, a large safe deposit box in her hands. She smiled, set it carefully on the table, and left.

"Would you like to be alone?" Malakai asked.

I shook my head. "It's fine. You were with them when they left this, weren't you?"

"Actually, I opened the box for them."

Nodding, I took in a breath and gingerly lifted the lid.

CHAPTER 17

Letting out a little gasp of surprise, I reached my hand out to remove the top item. It was an envelope, with my name scrawled across the top in an unfamiliar print. It was elegant and graceful, and I knew instinctively it was my mother's.

One by one, I took the contents out and laid them across the table. There were photos, jewelry, a couple books and a few other trinkets. Tears welled in my eyes as I stared unblinking at the tiny collection.

"Is there, perhaps, a small box or bag we could have to carry these home?" Tristan asked.

"Yes, of course," Malakai answered immediately and left the room.

"Home," I whispered, still staring. Where was home?

When Tristan spoke, there was an odd edge to his voice. "You will return with me, will you not?"

I glanced up at him now, and his eyes were so dark they were black. "You want me to?" I said uncertainly.

He laughed, the sound loud and surprising in the tiny room. I couldn't remember ever hearing him sound so carefree.

"Of course, I do. My home is yours. I wish never to leave you." His tone abruptly turned serious, and I couldn't look away from him. The tears were brimming again, but this time it wasn't over my parent's gift.

We continued to stare at one another before a gentle clearing of a throat snapped us out. "Forgive me," Malakai said. "Here is a box for your things."

"Thank you," I told him, taking the small cardboard box and quickly looking at the items again. Methodically I packed them in for the return trip. Later, I would look at them more closely.

"There is also the matter of the money," he reminded me when I was finished.

"Oh," I said, my mind a little scattered. "Could I keep it here for now?" I had almost forgotten it. It should be put in an account for the baby, I thought now. My hand covered the small mound subconsciously.

"Of course," he smiled. "Anytime you wish to make other arrangements, anyone here at the bank, or myself, will be able to help you."

I nodded. Tristan held the box in one hand and my hand in the other. He led me out, Malakai on our heels.

"It was so nice to meet you," I said to him when we reached the front door. "Thank you."

He shook my hand and smiled warmly. "It was my pleasure. Please, come back anytime." Switching his grip to Tristan's now free hand, he repeated, "Anytime."

The sun had dipped below the horizon, turning the sky into a mesh of pinks and purples. I sat on the steps of the plane, realizing how out of place the beauty in the sky was with the matter that had to be attended to.

Tristan knelt before me, cupping one hand against the side of my face. "I swear I will return to you. Before, I went in blind, but now I know what I'm up against. Plus, I have help."

I nodded. I knew all that. It didn't seem to matter to my pounding heart.

"I love you, Reya Tane."

Tears brimmed again. All these emotions were so overpowering, I sincerely hoped it was the pregnancy and not a new normal.

That was the first time that Tristan had told me he loved me. Somehow, I knew it. I knew it the first time I saw him, in our dreamland.

"And I love you, Tristan Amiri." It didn't take much to lean in so our lips could touch. Making eye contact again, I used my firmest voice. "You *will* come back to me."

"Always," he responded, and pulled me in for another kiss. This one wasn't so short, and it took the clearing of a throat to break us apart.

I looked up, annoyed, at Jared. He just grinned back, before turning a sober look to Tristan.

"It's time."

Tristan nodded once, pressed his lips to mine once more and stood, joining Jared at the rental truck.

There was an arsenal in the trunk, but I didn't want to know specifics. I was a healer, not a hurter, but I knew what it would take to free those poor men who were being held prisoner.

Aden drove the truck while Tristan and Jared disappeared into the night. The plan was for Tristan and Jared to go in and free the men first, then use the truck to bring the prisoners back to the airport. After I did what I could for them, they would be transferred to a hospital.

Gary stuck with me, my only company to wait out the nerve-wracking evening.

"Tell me about yourself," I asked him, needing a distraction.

"What would you like to know?" He wondered.

Shrugging, I asked the first question that came to mind. "How did you decide to become a pilot?"

Gary leaned back on the seat, making himself comfortable. I sat cross legged, my hands wrapped around my middle, staring out the window.

"When I was 18 I joined the military," Gary told me. "Had an aptitude for flying. Once I was out, I was hired on a commercial airline, but it didn't suit me. So, I went into the private sector."

"Is that how you met Jared?"

"No," Gary grinned at the memory. "We met long before that. He's actually the reason I joined the military, straightened myself out. If it wasn't for him, I'd likely have ended up in jail."

"How much do you know about... his lifestyle?"

Gary leaned forward, pulling out a secret drawer from beneath the seat. To my surprise, it was temperature controlled, and filled to the brim with blood bags.

"Enough," was his answer.

Reya, the voice calmed all my nerves in an instant. *We have arrived at the camp.*

What is it? I asked him, sensing a hesitation in his words.

It's deserted.

The captives are gone? I asked, panicked.

No, he told me. *Everyone else.*

"Gary," I spoke aloud, my heart in my throat. "Something's wrong."

He was instantly on his feet, alert. "What is it?"

"There's no one at the camp besides the captives," I explained, searching out the windows myself. I had a bad feeling about this. A very bad feeling.

Without questioning how I knew this, Gary began strapping weapons to himself, his moves efficient. I watched helplessly, knowing I wouldn't have the capacity to use a gun.

Instead, I began closing all the windows on the plane. If there was someone watching, I didn't want to make it easy for them.

"Put this on," Gary ordered me, handing me a vest.

"Bullet proof?" I asked. He nodded.

As I began to slip the vest on, an explosion rocked the plane. I fell to the floor, catching myself on my palms. Gary was thrown against the wall, letting loose with a string of curses.

Attempting to rise to my feet, Gary was suddenly beside me, yanking me down. "Stay down," he ordered, punctuating his actions.

While Gary approached a window to assess the situation, I searched the plane, making sure it was still intact. Whatever had exploded seemed like it was far enough away that it didn't affect the plane directly.

"We're surrounded." Gary uttered the words starkly, and I felt a well of fear bubble up.

Tristan, I said his name like the lifeline it was. *We're under attack. The plane has been surrounded. There was an explosion, but we're both fine.*

A growl erupted in my mind, and it took several seconds before anything comprehensible came through. *Tell me everything. How many are there? What kind of weapons?*

"Gary," I spoke as calmly as I was able. "How many are there? What kinds of weapons do they have?"

"I see four approaching this side. Semi-automatic weapons, full combat gear. Six more in hiding that I can pick out. Same on the other side of the plane."

I relayed this information to Tristan while I slipped on the vest that had been thrown from my hands during the explosion.

"Gary, where's your vest?" I asked, but before he could reply, the door exploded off its hinges.

We were both thrown again, and this time I was on my back, the breath knocked out of me and a shrill ringing in my ears.

Men boarded the plane, guns leading the way. Gary began firing from his prone position on the floor, and two of the men crumpled before I saw Gary jerk back.

No! I screamed silently. Then, two more men were on top of me, grabbing me by my shoulders and hauling me to my feet. They carried me off the plane, which was no easy task through the small opening that had been blown through the hatch.

They stood me on the tarmac, gripping my wrists behind my back at an angle that was shooting pains up to my shoulders. A group approached us, a tight huddle protecting one man.

"Ah, Ms. Tane. How lovely to see you again."

Glaring, struggling against the hands restraining my wrists, I spit out, "What do you want?"

Donovan laughed, a sardonic sound that grated on me. His hands spread before him, as if the answer was obvious. "Why, what I've always wanted. You, your child. And, of course, your friends."

I was shaking with fury at his words, at the situation he'd put me in. Images flitted through my mind; the sight of Tristan in chains, tortured, the innocent men in the camp who were undergoing the same treatment. Countless others that didn't make it. My child's future.

It started in the pit of my stomach, a burning fire that grew until it felt as if there were sparks shooting out of my fingertips, crackling through my hair. I heard a yelp of pain and suddenly my wrists were released, my arms rising to my sides of their own accord.

My only focus was on Donovan. His eyes widened and, too late, began stumbling backwards.

The energy burst from me, all my anger and frustration of being helpless rolled out like a maelstrom. Everyone in a 20-foot radius flew back, landing hard several feet from where they stood. Instead of feeling drained, every inch of my skin still crackled with barely contained power.

Moving forward, my focus unwavering as I stalked towards Donovan, I paused when I towered over him.

"Goodbye, Donovan," I growled, raising my hand back.

Just as I began to lower it towards my target, Donovan's heart, I was restrained once again. With an aggravated growl, I spun, finding myself trapped against a large, hard chest.

"It's enough, *tau o te ate*. It is done."

Shaking, I protested. "No."

A hand soothed down my hair, releasing sparks as if they were nothing more than static. "You are not a killer, Reya. This is not for you to do."

His words, whispered against my temple, struck a chord in me. I collapsed against him, feeling the power reign in as tears escaped. Sagging, I wept for what I had almost done.

Pressing his hand against the back of my head, shielding me from the destruction I'd wrought, Tristan led me back towards the plane. In the distance I saw Jared come upon the scene of destruction.

With a gasp, I pulled away from Tristan. "Gary!"

Before he could respond I began to run towards the plane, cursing myself for thinking of myself first and not the injured man who had tried to save me.

He was lying in the same spot on the plane, eyes closed. Knowing Tristan was on my heels, I began to explain as I knelt beside the dying man.

"They blew in the door," I explained. "Gary tried to stop them, dropped those two," I gestured to the bodies in the aisle.

While I spoke, my hands were running over Gary, his wound. The bullet went through close to his heart, but missed, though it hit an artery. Closing my eyes, I focused, knowing Tristan would protect me. The heat built, transferred while I chanted.

The bullet wormed its way free and I immediately pressed the cloth to the wound. Tristan was there, pressing firmly to free my hands. With the bullet removed, it was time to reattach torn tissue. The energy pouring from me was a pure white, healing light.

Gary coughed, his eyes rolling in an attempt to open.

"Shh, Gary, stay still. You were injured, and I need you to stay still while I heal you."

He coughed again, his head turning to the side while blood poured from his mouth. My terrified gaze switched to Tristan for the barest moment, and I saw the same knowledge in his eyes. Gary had blood in his lungs. He was dying.

CHAPTER 18

"I can't do this alone," I told Tristan, sorrow lining my tone.

"You don't have to. I am here."

"As am I," a new voice entered.

I looked up, bewildered.

"Jace," I heard Tristan greet the man with relief.

Jace knelt opposite me, giving me a nod. We began to work in tandem; I continued with the torn artery and surrounding tissue, Jace began to work on his injured lung.

Jace's energy was different than my own, harder but still pure. I had never met another like me, but now wasn't the time for questions. I filed away my observations somewhere in the back of my mind while I continued to work at saving Gary's life.

Dimly I was aware of the return of Aden, but I didn't look up or acknowledge him, or Jared as he silently removed the bodies from the plane.

Finally, I completed my part. I double and triple checked, being sure every detail was correct. Jace was still working, and without fully knowing what I was doing, I transferred my energy to him.

The combined power glowed brightly, and vaguely I wondered if any emergency vehicles had come to the small airport, considering the explosions, and how we would explain not only the battle scene, but also the display of power.

When Jace reeled in his power I did the same, and we both sat back, exhausted. Tristan was there immediately, holding my weight.

Jace gave me a once over. "You should allow me to examine you."

My eyes widened, though I shouldn't have been surprised. When I'd linked my energy to his, we'd formed a connection, opening ourselves up to the other. He would know about the baby.

"No, I'm fine. Perhaps we should get out of here?"

I shot my eyes towards Tristan quickly, hoping Jace would understand. Though his eyes narrowed imperceptibly, he nodded. I sighed with relief.

"I plan to accompany you back. You've used a lot of power today, and I would feel better if I could examine you then."

Nodding, I avoided Tristan's worried look.

Somehow Jared had commandeered another plane, and he reappeared now, lifting Gary carefully, bringing him on the new plane first. There was blood streaked across the floor.

"Jared will take care of things, *tau o te ate*. Let's get you on the plane also."

"I'll stay and clear things up here," Jared told us from the tarmac.

"I will help, then I will come visit your home," Jace added, speaking to Tristan. He gave me a meaningful look. I gave him a small nod, acknowledging his unspoken command.

Allowing Tristan to lead me, I stepped off the plane. The bodies of Donovan and his men were gone, and I presumed Jared and Aden had done something with them while I'd been working on Gary. At this point, I didn't want to know the specifics.

We stepped onto the new plane, sitting on one of the long benches. It wasn't as cozy as Gary's plane had been, but it would get us home.

"Where are all the men?" I asked Tristan, gripping his hand tightly. "I need to help them."

"You will do no such thing right now," Tristan amended. "Jace will see to them. Aden drove them here in the truck, they will be looked at now."

I acquiesced, knowing it was futile to argue with him at this point. Tristan coaxed me into laying down, my head pillowed in his lap, obviously concerned over Jace's words. I complied, partly not to argue but mostly because I was exhausted. Before we even took off, I was asleep.

When I woke, I was in Tristan's bed with just a dim light showing through the curtains. Since I was wearing a soft cotton nightgown, and not the dark clothes I remembered, I guessed Tristan had dressed me. He wasn't beside me, so I took the time to stretch and self-evaluate. Everything was just a little sore, but not unusual. I placed both hands on the slight bump of my stomach, knowing it was time to tell Tristan the truth.

Swinging both legs off the bed, I went in search of him. It surprised me not to find him next to me, but it was also difficult to tell how long I'd been asleep.

Roaming the still unfamiliar house, I stopped first in the kitchen and inhaled deeply, appreciating the aroma coming from whatever was simmering on the stove. He wasn't around, so I continued on in my search.

My bare feet padded silently across the smooth marble floors as I ventured into one room after another, each one taking my breath away. One of my favorite things was the large windows in each room, bringing the beautiful surroundings in.

Finally, I came upon a room, that, when I stood in the doorway, made me gasp aloud. This was the library Jared had told me of, and not only was it gorgeous with its two-story shelves, marble fireplace and cozy reading chairs, it was completely filled with books.

Tristan was there, before the fire, and he turned at my entrance. The room was cooled enough that the fire didn't seem out of place.

"Good evening," he spoke, assessing me from across the room.

"Evening?" I asked. "Did I sleep all day, then?"

He smiled and it made my heart beat faster. "You did. We arrived back in the early morning. I enjoyed changing you out of those dreary clothes."

A blush stole up my neck.

"How's Gary?" I asked in an attempt to distract him.

"Recovering, thanks to you. Aden brought him directly to the hospital when we arrived. Jared and Jace returned this afternoon, and all the men we rescued are also in recovery."

I let out a breath. "That's good news."

The distraction was done. He moved then, standing in front of me, a finger skimming down the material of the nightgown. It was very feminine, white and flowing. His thumb brushed across my skin and my entire body reacted.

"Yes, much better," he murmured. He kissed me then, his hands trapping my face. Instinctively, my hands grasped his arms while my body pressed itself against his.

One arm wrapped itself around my back, lifting me so my legs wrapped around his waist. We moved, though I hardly noticed, until we were in front of the fire. A large, soft rug covered the floor there and he set me down on it gently. His hands, slightly rough, moved across my body and I ached for more. Quickly he disposed of the nightgown, stretching me out on the rug for his full viewing.

He knelt above me, devouring me with his eyes. My body still reached toward him, ached for him, but I remained still, knowing it was what he wanted.

"You are truly beautiful, *tau o te ate*. Mesmerizing."

I shivered at the compliments, needing him.

"Tristan? What does *tau o te ate* really mean?"

He leaned in close, his body hovering just above my own, his lips just a scant distance away. "Soul mate. Lover. *Mine*," he finished with a growl, his lips meeting mine once again.

There was nothing gentle now, just pure need. My hands ripped at his clothing, needing to feel his skin against mine. His hands ran over every inch of my body with his mouth following suit. I squirmed with a need I'd never known, one that I knew I'd spend eternity attempting to satiate.

"Tristan," his name came out as a plea, a talisman in the storm he was creating, until we both shuddered in release.

Pulling his head back to look into my eyes, Tristan kissed me again, long and deep. In a quick move, he rolled to his back, bringing me on top of him so his weight wasn't crushing me.

I sighed happily, snuggling into him. This was heaven, right here in Tristan's arms. I would never have enough of this.

"Are you hungry?" He spoke quietly after several minutes.

I smiled into his chest. "Yes, actually. Starved."

Carefully he rolled me onto my back again. "Stay here," he told me sternly.

I did as I was told, for a moment. Sitting up carefully, I cast about for my discarded nightgown, spying it by the doorway. The time between wearing it and not wearing it had become slightly fuzzy. Standing then, I stretched with my hands reaching up, twisting my body to each side and enjoying the soreness of muscles I hadn't really ever used before.

Pulling the nightgown back into place, I began to wander around the room, touching a delicate finger to a book title here and there. There were several first edition classics, and it astounded me when I realized these were more than likely not acquired as antiques.

"You do not listen very well." Tristan sounded amused.

Grinning over at him, I replaced the novel that I'd been holding in my hand. "You might as well get used to that."

He shook his head and set the tray of food down on a small table between the overstuffed chairs. Following the delicious aroma, I walked over to him and breathed in appreciatively. "So, you *can* cook," I commented.

"Of course," he responded, as if the mere thought of me doubting his ability was ridiculous.

"Tristan," I said his name quietly, placing an arm on his bicep. "There's something I need to tell you."

"What is it, *tau o te ate*?" he turned, immediately concerned.

"It's just... well... I'm... I mean, *we're*..." I took a deep breath and let it out in a rush. "We're having a baby."

He was stunned, his body completely still. As he continued to stare at me, I worried he was going into shock.

"Tristan?" I squeezed his arm gently. "Please, say something," I begged.

"How could you know? It would only be a couple of days..." Tristan trailed off, looking utterly bewildered.

"Well, here's the thing," I began, a self-deprecating smile in place. "Remember the night, in our dream world?"

If it was possible for Tristan to look more startled, he managed it. "How is that possible?" His voice was barely above a whisper.

"Sit down," I nudged him gently into the chair behind him, kneeling at his feet, keeping hold of his hands. "Tristan, look at me. I know this is a shock. Believe me, it was even more so for me, since I didn't remember that night at first. But, that doesn't mean it's not true."

"A baby," he murmured, then finally focused on me. "That's amazing, Reya."

"Is it?" I smiled nervously.

"Yes, of course! Are you not excited?"

"I'm not sure I've had time to be excited," I told him honestly.

His smile quickly disappeared. "This is the real reason you made the trip to Ayers Rock. To find out who your family was."

I nodded, surprised he'd pieced that together so quickly. Pulling me into his lap, Tristan kissed me even more gently than before, resting a hand against my middle.

"A baby," he spoke in awe. "Our baby."

When his eyes met mine again, they were lit with pure joy. Something settled within me at his expression, something I desperately needed.

"I will call for Jace immediately," Tristan announced. "You need to be checked. Do you need to lay down? Rest more?"

I laughed, the most carefree laugh I think I'd ever had. "I'm pregnant, not sick," I told him. "Though, I would like to eat. This smells amazing. And, before you call Jace, I'd like to be wearing something a little less see-through."

Tristan grinned then, kissing me one more time, before setting me in my own chair and uncovering a bowl of steaming stew that had my mouth watering.

CHAPTER 19

When Jace arrived, I was watching Tristan clean up from dinner. I'd changed into a sundress and propped myself on the counter, my bare feet dangling. Though I'd attempted to *help* him clean up, watching was all that I was allowed to do.

I settled on the couch, Jace in a chair beside me. Tristan stood at the back of the couch, clasping my hand in his.

"You haven't done this yourself?" Jace asked.

Startled, I answered him, "No. It never occurred to me to try this on myself."

Jace smirked. "I'll be sticking around here for a while," he reminded me. "We can train together. The amount that you've learned on your own is actually rather impressive."

"She is amazing," Tristan agreed, smiling down at me.

Rolling my eyes, I teased, "You have to say that."

"Jared has told me a little about your family. Now that he knows your parents' names, he's been able to confirm you are, in fact, related."

"I didn't think male foreseers were anything more than legend," Tristan murmured, as if to himself.

The thought made me want to laugh. "What, around here, isn't legend?"

"Elementals have their own legends," Tristan winked at me. "We used to have a close-knit community here. Much of that has been lost. That's why Jared, Jace and I have stuck together. Our families were also close."

"I'd like to hear more about that," I told him.

"After the exam, perhaps when Jared and Aden arrive," Jace prompted.

Nodding, I allowed him to use his special healing powers to tell me how my baby was. I felt a warm heat spreading across my midsection, and after several minutes of silence, Jace focused back on me.

"They're doing fine," he told me. "Completely healthy. It seems you're right around 11 weeks."

"They're?" I squeaked out. "*They're* doing well?"

Tristan smiled proudly. "Twins?"

Jace nodded. "Would you like to know the sexes?"

My eyes met Tristan's and I nodded.

"One boy, one girl," he told us.

My hands wrapped around my stomach, which had already started to protrude. "Hi, babies," I said softly.

"It's twins!" Jared's voice floated over to us from the kitchen.

He and Aden had let themselves in, and to my surprise and delight, he produced a handful of balloons.

"Congratulations, officially. And now that we know there's one of each, be prepared to be spoiled with lots and lots of gifts," Jared grinned widely at me.

"You'll have to forgive Jared's exuberance," Jace's brow rose. "It's been quite some time since there's been children around here."

Sitting up, I accepted the balloons, leaning forward to set them on the table. Jared, or at least someone at the store, had had the forethought to tie a weight to the bottom so they didn't just float to the ceiling.

"Thank you, so much," I told Jared.

Tristan came to sit beside me, and gestured for the others to sit also.

"We have much to discuss," Tristan began. "Donovan and his men have been arrested, and we'll need to get in and question them."

"Everyone is recovering well," Jared continued, "though three of them are still unconscious from the drug. Which brings us to another point; since Donovan knew we were coming, all of their research had been cleared from the sight."

I was disappointed by this, but all was not lost. Clearing my throat, I spoke up, "I have a small vial of Tristan's blood from when he was infected. The pure form of the drug would have been better to work with, but it gives us a starting point."

"Good thinking," Jace answered me. "I'd be happy to look at it with you. I've got a small lab on my property you are welcome to use."

Tristan's arm tightened slightly around me, and I looked up into his eyes.

What is it? I asked him.

I just want to make sure you get proper rest, that is all.

Smirking, I answered, *You're not going to be jealous if I spend all my time with Jace, are you?*

That is not what this is about.

Don't worry, macho man. I want you with me as much as possible.

Putting my attention back on the group, I looked at Aden. "What's your plan now? Will you stick around here?"

Aden looked uncomfortable briefly before responding. "I don't believe this camp was the only one Donovan's group had. I have some leads from my time there, and that's the second reason we'd like to question the men that have been arrested. Jared and I plan on shutting them all down."

"That's so dangerous," my worried gaze stayed on Aden.

"That's true, and it brings me to my next point," Aden cleared his throat before meeting each man's gaze individually. "I'd like to be changed."

Utter silence met his request. I could see Jared had already made his decision, but his eyes were on Tristan, as were Jace's. Though it was never said aloud, I realized now that Tristan was, for all intents and purposes, the leader of this small group. If he disagreed with this, the others would follow him.

Finally, Tristan nodded. "This is truly what you want?"

Aden nodded. "Yes."

"There are many benefits to this life, but it is not always easy. You must always be vigilant, both with your safety and keeping our existence from the human world. And those shadow men that took your sister, they were once like us," Tristan added, wanting to drive the point home. "Power, when not wielded properly, can take over. First, they lose their minds to it, then, their souls. Will you be strong enough to fight this?"

Aden gulped, then nodded again. "Yes."

"It will be done."

Relaxing now, Aden continued on, "To fully answer your question, Reya, my ultimate goal is to find my sister. Jared has agreed to help me."

"We will, too," I answered for myself and Tristan.

"As will I," Jace spoke up.

"Thank you, all," Aden seemed overcome by emotion. "But, our first order of business is shutting down these camps."

"Jace, Reya, the sooner you can come up with a cure to this drug, the better."

We both nodded at Jared.

"When will you be questioning Donovan?" I asked.

"Today," Jared answered.

"Are you prepared to go through the change now?" Tristan asked Aden. "You will be unconscious from three to five days. Though I did not go through it myself, I know it is not... pleasant."

I winced, looking up at Tristan again. He seemed genuinely concerned about putting Aden through this.

"Why don't we wait until after we question the men," Aden answered slowly. "Perhaps then we can have a good plan in place before I undergo the change."

"You will not wake up with your full powers," Tristan explained, "So it may be a while before you will be a help to Jared."

Aden and Jared shared a look. "I understand," Aden assured us. "This is something I need to do."

"You will stay here while you recover," Tristan decided. "That way you will have both myself and Reya to look after you."

"Thank you," Aden said quietly.

"Okay, on to fun stuff," I told them, smiling. "Tell me about your families, how it used to be."

Jared looked confused for a moment before Jace filled him in. "We were telling Reya about the tight knit community we used to have, when we were young."

"How long ago, exactly, was that?" I asked.

"The three of us were born in the mid-1800's," Jared told me with a grin.

Aden and I shared a look, and I reminded myself to breathe. "Okay, then," I rearranged my thoughts. "Tell me about your families."

"We were each born as a set of twins," Jace picked up the story. "Twins are normal for Elementals. I believe because of our longevity, children are rare, but when one of us does conceive..." He trailed off, gesturing towards my mid-section. "Tristan and I each lost our twin," he continued, sadly.

At this I squeezed Tristan's hand, lending him my support.

"We each had a close relationship with our sibling," Jared told me. "Hugh and I are still close, though he's in America at the moment. There are some pretty cool things about the relationship between twins. For one, which you know, Reya, we can speak telepathically. We also have the ability to combine our power."

"I'm not a twin," I mused aloud.

"I have a theory on that," Jace spoke up. "I believe that's because of your dad."

"My dad?"

"Yes," Jace continued. "A male foreseer is extremely rare. So much so, that the three of us have never met one in our lifetime. Tristan told you earlier that we have our own legends, and this was one of them."

"What do the legends say?" I asked in a low voice.

"They mostly speak of his powers," Jace told me. "They were said to be unparalleled. There are also some things that were said of their children."

Looking between the men in the room, I finally asked, "What was said?"

Tristan picked up the story. "Unlike other Elementals, it was said male foreseers were only able to conceive once, but that their child would have the combined power of their parents."

I tried to digest this information. "Does that mean... do you think I could see the future?"

"It's possible," Tristan told me. "After speaking with Malakai, it became clear you possess some of the abilities of your mother, along with your own healing power. Now that you know what you are, and are feeding properly, who knows what else you might be able to do?"

Letting out a breath, my only response to this was, "Wow."

"I can see I was wasting your potential with basic element manipulation," Jared teased.

"That reminds me," I looked to Jared. "When you were first explaining all this to Aden and me, you mentioned increased hearing, speed, shifting- I can't do any of that."

"Are you sure?" Jace asked gently. "If you have as much power as we believe you do, perhaps you learned to suppress it all at a young age. You traveled in your dreams, but couldn't remember during the day. To me, that sounds like your conscious was suppressing what your subconscious knows. Tell me about the first times you used your healing powers."

Relaying the story of Isy's broken leg, I watched as the expressions on the others' faces became more and more amazed.

"I think you need to practice," Jace finally spoke after I'd finished. "With Tristan's help, I believe you can unlock all of your potential."

Jared and Aden stood then, preparing to leave to question Donovan's men. Jace joined them, leaving me alone with Tristan and my thoughts.

"Well?" I asked him. "Up for a little practice?"

Bringing my hand to his lips, he answered, "Of course, *tau o te ate.*"

CHAPTER 20

"There is somewhere I would like to show you," Tristan said as we stood in the grass just outside the kitchen door.

Smiling over at him, I said, "I'm game."

"We can try… running there," Tristan watched me carefully.

"Like, as an animal?" I verified.

His grin was my answer.

"All right," I agreed. "Tell me what to do."

"First, you'll want to undress," Tristan told me, the grin still very apparent.

"What?" I exclaimed. "You're kidding, right?"

"No," Tristan told me. "Our bodies change, but our clothes do not. Eventually you will be able to shift into molecules as small as the air before you take on the shape of an animal, and therefore not ripping your clothes, but we will save that for our second lesson."

I was staring at him with my mouth agape as he said all this. Realizing he wasn't kidding, I slowly removed my dress, feeling very self-conscious. When Tristan began removing his own clothes, I felt my mouth go dry.

"You can't possibly expect me to focus *now*," I teased.

"Pay attention now, and I shall reward you later," he replied, and I felt the heat rise from the soles of my feet right into my cheeks.

Closing his eyes, Tristan took a deep breath in. "Everything we do, we do with our minds. Build the image you want to become in your mind first. Choose an animal you are familiar with. What would you like?"

"Um…" I debated. "A cat. Something fast."

"Let's try for a panther," Tristan suggested. "Imagine each part, the sleek black fur, the watchful eyes. Breathe deep, and allow your mind to shed your current body."

Closing my eyes, I did as he asked. When I felt a shimmer in the air, I popped my eyes open to watch as his form wavered, then shrank, becoming the panther.

With a gasp, I reached a hand out, allowing my fingers to sink into the soft fur. He let out a purr, wrapping his lithe body around my legs. Then, he stood back, watching me. I understood.

Closing my eyes again, I built the image in my mind. Concentrating hard, I felt the sensation first from the pit of my stomach, before I felt as if I were falling forward. Instead of hitting the ground, I felt weightless, each of my limbs rising from the ground. My body floated apart before being slammed back together.

Opening my eyes, I let out a noise that came out as a huff, my vocal chords diminished in the form of the panther. My head whipped to the side, seeking out my mate, and it seemed completely natural to rub my body against his.

Tristan's cat pushed his head against mine, then in a sudden move, sprang away, racing towards the edge of the tree. My cat followed suit, paws light and quick as they hit the ground, one after the other. Easily catching up to Tristan, I let him lead, enjoying the sheer freedom of the run.

It didn't take long until we were in deep woods, and I could sense water nearby. The scene abruptly became achingly familiar.

My cat paused with a start, and this time when I let out a gasp, it was with my own voice. I'd been shocked back into my own form.

Tristan appeared before me, amusement plastered on his features.

"Your concentration broke," Tristan chided.

"This is our place," I breathed, ignoring his chastisement. "You said you lived here, I just... I didn't realize..."

It was so beautiful, my heart actually ached. Trees swayed gently in the breeze, the trickling of water a soothing chorus.

"Let's walk to the river," Tristan said quietly, reaching for my hand.

After several steps, he paused, releasing my hand to walk to a circle of trees. To my surprise, he uncovered a box, opening it to reveal clothing.

Handing me a large shirt, he pulled on a pair of pants for himself. "I thought you might be more comfortable," he told me.

"Thank you," I responded, relieved. Pulling the shirt over my head, it hung down almost to my knees.

"I will be sure to add your own clothing to each of my caches," Tristan promised me.

We continued towards the river, the path a familiar one from my dreams. Once we reached the shore, we stood together, Tristan standing at my back with his arms wrapped around my waist.

"Let's start simple," he whispered into my ear. I had to close my eyes to concentrate. "Listen to the wind through the trees. There is a bird chirping. Imagine a volume dial, like on a radio, that controls your hearing. Turn it up slowly, tell me what you hear."

With my eyes still closed, I did as he asked. Soon, I could hear each individual bird, their songs unique. A light scratching of little critters running up the trees. Further still, a fluttering *thump, thump*. A heartbeat, of a very large bird.

"There's some kind of large bird half a mile that way," I pointed, opening my eyes to look up at Tristan. "Am I right?"

"That's correct," he smiled, then let out an interesting whistle bordering on a croak. Just a couple of minutes later, a majestic white bird landed in the tree nearest us.

Gasping, I reached out a hand as if to stroke it.

"This is kōtuku, a white heron," Tristan whispered into my ear again. "It is indigenous to New Zealand, but has become a rare sight. They became nearly extinct, until Waitangiroto Nature Reserve began protecting them."

"That's incredible," I breathed as the majestic bird took flight once again.

"You're doing very well," Tristan complimented me.

"I've been thinking a lot about what Jared and Jace talked about," I told him. "That either my parents helped me suppress my powers, or I did it myself to fit in. When Donovan attacked me at the airport, it was like all the restraint I'd had exploded, and I could almost see the magic inside me."

"I think we could all see the magic, it was sparking from your hair."

Nudging him, I responded, "You know what I mean."

"Jace believes you've had your powers since such a young age you don't remember even suppressing them. It is actually extremely rare for an Elemental to come into their powers before their twenty-fifth year," Tristan told me. "Our parents still trained us to be ready, to understand how to handle them, but we typically do not fully develop until around our mid-twenties."

"How old were you?" I asked out of curiosity.

"I was very young," Tristan said in a matter of fact tone, and I could detect no pride in his words. "My mother told me when she was pregnant with my sister and myself, she would feel incredible pain, and our healer at the time came to realize I was shifting inside the womb."

My mouth dropped open, and I instinctually wrapped my arms around my own stomach. "Our kids won't do that, will they?" I looked up at him with a lopsided grin.

"Let us hope not," Tristan answered.

Suddenly, Tristan cocked his head to the side as if he was listening intently. Realizing that was exactly what he was doing, I sent out my own senses, trying to pinpoint what had made Tristan go so still.

Faintly, I could hear Jared's voice, but I couldn't make out what he was saying. Tristan stiffened, pulling me close to him again.

"We need to go. Now."

"What's going on?" I asked, frightened now, but I didn't get an answer.

Tristan wrapped his arms around me tight, lifting me off the ground, and then he was running. He was moving so fast, I had to tuck my head into his shoulder to stop the wave of dizziness. I was sure it was only the pregnancy that was causing my queasiness, and not the blinding speed Tristan displayed.

What's going on? What is it? I pushed the questions into his mind, afraid to open my mouth.

At first, I wasn't sure he was going to answer. When he did, I felt chilled down to my bones. *Donovan's escaped.*

Just a couple minutes after we'd started running, we slowed, back on Tristan's land. Jared and Aden were already there, and Jace looked as if he were scouting the perimeter.

"We found out when we arrived at the station," Jared began explaining immediately. "One of the guards was on his payroll."

"Get inside," Tristan urged me.

I was conflicted. My natural response was to help- though with what, I wasn't entirely sure- but it wasn't only my life I had to think about anymore. My children came first.

Any decision I'd come to became a moot point.

There was a *pop, pop, pop* in rapid succession, and I stared out over the yard, horrified. Tristan, Jared and Jace were all on the ground, their life-giving blood leaking into the earth.

Aden was closest to me, his body alert, attempting to shield mine. My heart was in my throat as I stared at Tristan's prone figure. Pure, unadulterated rage surged through my system until I saw red.

Mother earth, strong and true. Protect your sons, protect your daughters. Heal their wounds, this I ask of you.

In a sudden surge of energy, my body was aglow with the sheer power of the earth. It radiated out from my skin like a shield, enveloping Aden in its warmth. Through my bare feet, I could feel the earth's pulse, succumbing to my will. Veins of warmth shot from my position to the three men that had become my family.

Soil grew up and around Tristan, Jared and Jace, encasing them in a protective shell. Through my connection, I felt the earth searching for the strongest minerals and herbs, sending their healing powers along the veins of warmth and directly into their bodies. Simultaneously, I sent my healing power to all three. Instead of the power feeling diminished, it merely grew to meet my need.

Ignoring the odd sensation of being in multiple places at once, I focused my thoughts on healing.

Blood escaped, be replaced. Metal intruding, return from whence you came.

Bullets, that had been embedded deep, suddenly lifted into the air, floating above the earthly cocoons. In a split second, they whizzed away, finding new homes in the men that had pulled the trigger.

Stitch and seal, what was once one become one again.

The three came back to consciousness with a gasp, still enveloped in the earth's healing arms.

Smooth the scars, release the pain. Mother Earth, I ask this in your name.

Her work done, Mother Earth slowly receded, releasing the men from her grasp.

Slowly, the men stood, looking around in a daze. Running at my full speed, I jumped into Tristan's arms.

"You're okay," I said through a barrage of kisses to his face. "You're okay."

His arms wrapped around me securely, holding me closely for a long while. "You will never cease to amaze me," he whispered into my ear.

I pulled back, tears in my eyes, and inspected his chest for myself to ensure there was no proof of the potentially mortal wound.

Ripping open his blood-stained shirt, I ran my hands carefully across the slightly reddened skin, on the last stages of mending.

Jace and Jared approached us then, clearly in awe.

"How did you *do* that?" Jace was the first to speak.

"I honestly have no idea," I told him. Then, looking around, I realized one of us was missing. "Where's Aden?"

They all looked around. He had been standing beside me while I'd been healing, but he was nowhere to be seen now.

On an unspoken command, we all turned and ran towards the line of trees. Expanding my hearing, I could hear a struggle, and I forced my legs to move even faster.

I realized, as my feet hit the ground, the earth was sending me messages. Listening to her, I turned and followed a direct path to Aden.

Donovan was there, in a small clearing, held to the ground by two small mounds that had risen up to cover his feet. That meant he was immobile- but he also had Aden.

Donovan held Aden in a death grip, a knife at his throat. We all paused, trying to assess the situation. What had Aden been thinking, coming after Donovan on his own?

"Release me, if you wish to keep your friend alive," Donovan demanded.

"Donovan," I brought his attention to me. "I will release you, but you must first let Aden go."

"You think I'm an idiot?" he sneered. "Release me first."

You've got this? I sent to Tristan.

I've got this.

"All right, Donovan. I'll release you."

Sending my energy into the earth, I asked for Donovan to be released. Reluctantly, the earth receded.

He immediately stumbled back, bringing Aden with him. I reached out as if to yank him away, but there was a restraining arm across my midsection. Jared.

"Donovan," I said firmly. "Release Aden now. I've done what you asked."

"Oh, no," Donovan said. "I'm not finished with you yet. It's you I want. You, and your child. I'll trade Aden's life... for yours."

With an inward gasp, I attempted to step forward again, but was held back once more.

"Reya, you're more important than me. There's no point. I'll gladly give my life for yours."

"No," I whispered, tears in my eyes. Then, stronger, "No, I won't let you do this."

While we were speaking, Tristan faded into the background, shifting into air molecules in order to sneak behind Donovan. I could sense him, whether through my new connection to the earth or my connection to Tristan as mates, I couldn't be sure. He was directly behind Donovan now, positioned for striking.

Not soon enough. Donovan realized what was happening, his eyes wide, searching the small clearing. "Where is he? What have you done?"

Tristan materialized then, and in a last-ditch effort, Donovan sliced the knife across Aden's throat.

CHAPTER 21

Aden's body dropped as Tristan's simply disappeared into Donovan. Jolting forward, I dropped to my knees beside Aden, pressing my hands to his wound. Jace was beside me in an instant, and I could already feel his healing powers coursing through Aden.

Tristan reappeared, and, as Jared dragged Donovan's body away, he knelt beside me. "He will not survive this as a human," Tristan told me gently. "We need to put him through the change."

With tear soaked eyes, I looked up into Tristan's beloved face. "What do I have to do?"

"Keep him alive," Tristan told me gruffly.

Taking Aden's wrist, Tristan brought it to his mouth, biting into the vein there. Ignoring the twist in my gut, I focused on lending Jace my energy while still clamping my hands on the wound on his throat.

"Stay with me, Aden." I chanted, hoping he could hear me.

When Tristan had taken enough, he slit open his own wrist. "Open his mouth," he instructed me.

"The wound… it needs to close," I told him.

Taking his hand back, Tristan nodded, trusting in me. Taking a deep breath, I let Jace continue working on the inner tissue while I worked on closing the skin.

I didn't know how long it took, but as soon as I was able, I opened my eyes and nodded at Tristan. "Now."

Without hesitation, Tristan re-opened the wound on his wrist and pressed it to Aden's mouth. The blood dripped in, but he wasn't swallowing.

With the tips of my fingers, I rubbed up and down Aden's throat, coaxing his reflexes. Time seemed to stand still as my positivity began to drop.

Then, he swallowed. Tristan and I worked in tandem while Jace continued to heal his wound. Jared was on alert, his duty to keep us safe.

It was a slow process without Aden having the ability to gulp in the blood, but eventually Tristan gave me a nod, signaling he had enough in his system.

Jace sat back then, paler than I'd ever seen him. "Let's get him comfortable."

Jared lifted Aden off the ground as if he weighed no more than a rag doll and began running towards Tristan's house.

He was placed in a guest room and, after making sure he was comfortable, I made a bowl of warm, soapy water. Grabbing several wash cloths, I cleaned him up best I could, at least removing all of the blood. Tristan left me only briefly, bringing me my own clothes, and a new outfit for Aden.

"Go, *tau o te ate*, and we will help Aden."

Nodding gratefully, I took the bundle Tristan handed me and went to our room. My plan was to only change clothes, but when I caught sight of myself in the mirror, I quickly decided a full shower was in order.

The hot spray felt good on my muscles, exhaustion settling in now that the rush of adrenaline had died down. Though staying in the warmth was tempting, I knew it wasn't a viable option. Instead, I moved quickly, dressing in the comfortable drawstring pants and soft cotton shirt Tristan had provided.

When I made it back to the guest room, only Jace and Tristan were still there.

"Where's Jared?" I asked quietly, brushing a hand across Aden's forehead. He felt warm, as if he were running a fever.

"It's the change," Tristan explained on seeing my concern. "The fever is the first to set in."

"Jared is back at the station," Jace answered my question. "We never actually got to talk to anyone earlier."

"Do you think they'll be more forthcoming now that Donovan…" I trailed off, unable to stomach the reality.

Tristan approached me, wrapping an arm around my waist. "It is not your fault, *tau o te ate*. Please do not blame yourself."

I nodded, unconvinced.

"But, yes, we believe they will be, now that they no longer have a leader," Jace answered. Then, he quietly asked, "Can we talk about what happened out there?"

Glancing over at him, I shrugged my shoulders. "I have no idea."

"You connected with the earth. We could all feel that. What was it like?"

"I asked her to protect you. She responded. I could feel the pulse of the earth through my feet, and it was as if I were getting messages from the earth itself. I knew exactly where each of you were, and what was wrong with you. I knew exactly where each of our enemies was, every animal, insect and mineral."

"That's incredible," Jace breathed out. "I've never heard of anything quite like that."

"It seems the stories are true," Tristan commented, watching me with pride in his eyes.

"You know," I pondered, "I was thinking about what you told me earlier, Tristan. About how you were able to shift when you were still in the womb. What if... what if these powers are not mine?"

Jace looked at me sharply. "You think it's your children?"

"According to your stories about male foreseers, I would have the powers of both my parents. I've never foreseen anything- at least not yet- but it seems I have traveled in my dreams. I also have my healing powers. It hardly seems fair I'd have yet another power."

Tristan and Jace exchanged a look, considering my words. "I suppose the only way we'll find out is once your children are born," Jace finally said. "With you two as parents, I don't think it would surprise me."

After I finished my inspection of Aden, Jace spoke again. "I'll stay here for now. You two go get some rest."

I knew he was concerned over me, and I didn't argue. Taking Tristan's hand, we walked slowly up the stairs and back into our room.

On a side table, the small cardboard box with the items from my parents sat. Slowly, I approached it, reaching in for the letter. I'd put this off long enough; it was time to see what my parents had written to me.

"Will you read it with me?" I asked Tristan, sinking onto the edge of the bed.

"If you wish, *tau o te ate.*"

"Please," I reached out, pulling him down beside me.

Sucking in a breath, I slid a finger under the flap of the envelope and removed the papers inside.

Dearest Reya,

I am so sorry to leave you like this. I know it feels as if we've abandoned you, but had we not done what we've done, you may never have met your mate.

Your father has seen many things about you, your life. You, along with Tristan, are meant for great things. You have one of the strongest healing abilities we've ever heard of, and, as the legends have foretold, you will have my abilities, along with your father's.

Foreseeing is not always the gift it may seem, and we have spelled you to suppress this power until you are ready. Enclosed are the instructions for you to release this ability, should you wish it. If and when you decide, seek out Malakai, he can assist you in this ceremony.

Your other powers that have been repressed are merely waiting, just under the surface, for you to believe in yourself.

We love you more than anything in the world. Forgive us for leaving you, as we never wanted to.

Always in your heart,

Mother

Tears in my eyes, I looked to Tristan, who was watching me carefully.

Cupping the side of my face, Tristan asked, "Are you all right?"

Sniffing, I nodded as he wiped an escaped tear from my cheek. "I'm not ready yet, but I'd like to perform the ceremony she spoke of," I told him.

He hesitated before agreeing. "If that is what you wish."

CHAPTER 22

Reya, 27 years old

"Why am I so nervous?" I asked Tristan. "It's not like there's a big crowd. This is silly. We don't need this, anyway. Let's just leave, go to our special place..."

"*Tau o te ate*, breathe. You must breathe for me."

Sucking in a mouthful of air, I let it out slowly. "Okay," I told him, "okay. I got this."

Tristan shook his head, a smile playing on his lips. "Facing down evil men, she does not rattle. Being the center of attention in our group of friends, and she balks."

Slapping him playfully on the arm, I rolled my eyes, but before I could respond, we were interrupted.

"What is this?" Isy's voice drifted to me from the door. I turned guiltily towards her. "You," she pointed at Tristan, "out. I need to get her ready."

At Tristan's amused look, I couldn't help but smile. Leave it to Isy to order Tristan around.

Before leaving, Tristan wrapped me in his arms, planting a kiss on me that had me aching for more. *Later*, he whispered into my mind. *I will be all yours.*

"Whew," Isy fanned herself when he'd left the room. "I'm having a hot flash over here."

I threw her a smile, then glanced at her arms nervously. There was certainly a lot of white bundled there.

"Come on," Isy piled the items on the bed before taking my hand, leading me to a small stool at the vanity. "Let's make you beautiful for your wedding."

Pulling my hair back into an intricate braid, Isy added fresh flowers until I felt like a fairy. I touched the petals of one flower lightly, smiling at the memory of my daughter lying in the grass in the yard, her favorite pass time. While I'd been pregnant, I'd felt a strong connection to the earth, but once the twins had been born, the connection had diminished, though not completely disappeared. The first time we'd brought the babies outside, it was easy to see my assumption had been correct- our daughter had a strong tie to the earth, so much so that when she laid in the grass, flowers would bloom all around her.

Our son's power was subtle, but just as strong. Whomever he was nearest, their own power would be amplified. I had a sneaking suspicion there would be much more he could do in time.

It would be interesting to watch how the two developed into their own. I was happy neither had shifted while in my womb, that sounded horribly painful, but it seemed they were both early developers, like their father.

Forty-five minutes later, I stood at the top of the stairs, staring down into the foyer, which was strewn with flowers. All I had to do was walk down the stairs and into the back yard.

Isy had already walked down the stairs, being my maid of honor. Jared- holding my son- and Jace would stand beside Tristan, while Aden- holding my daughter- would stand beside Isy.

Glancing over at Ben, I wrapped my hand through the crook of his arm.

"Thank you for being here," I told him.

"My pleasure, Reya," he patted my hand. "It's a beautiful place. And I don't have to ask if you're happy, I can see it."

Tears sprang to my eyes, and I fought them. Isy had spent way too much time on my make-up for me to ruin it.

"I am happy," I told Ben. "I have my whole family here."

I squeezed his arm and we shared a smile.

"Ready?" he asked.

Nodding, I took the first step down the stairs.

When we walked through the door, the first thing I noticed was the small fire pit Tristan had created. It was tradition to light a fire in order to welcome the spirit of our ancestors to the ceremony. Circled around the fire I saw Jared and Jace standing together, with Aden and Isy opposite, while Matt and Ben's wife, Teresa, rounded out the group. Malakai had agreed to officiate, and his wife stood near him. It was a small gathering, but it held all the people dearest to me.

Approaching the center, Ben transferred my hand to Tristan, clapping him on the shoulder before taking his place beside Matt.

"We come together today to bless the union of Tristan Amiri and Reya Tane," Malakai began, then dived into what Tristan had told me would be a traditional Elemental ceremony.

"Since ancient times, people have communed with nature to learn more about themselves. Since it is within nature that we all abide, we ask for Reya and Tristan the blessings of Nature's Elements; Air, Fire, Water and Earth. We do this that they may fully come to understand the lessons each element has to offer. The attributes of which are examples of those aspects they mirror, not only within divinity, but within ourselves as well."

"We ask the Spirits of Air to keep open the lines of communication between this couple. May their future be as bright as the dawn on the horizon. As Air flows freely to and from and through us all, may their hearts and minds and souls come to know the world and each other in this manner. Seeing not only with their eyes, may they together grow wise with wisdom."

A gentle breeze wrapped around us as Malakai spoke, reminding me of the sheer power of nature.

"Spirits of Fire, we ask that Reya and Tristan's passion for each other and for life itself remain ever strong and vital, fortifying each day with a vibrancy rooted in boldness, and courage. As Fire clears the way for new growth, may they know that this power is theirs: to create change and bring about the richness and quality that comes with a true love of life."

The bonfire Tristan had built grew larger, swelling in heat to remind us of its presence.

"We ask the Spirits of Water, that their love for each other and the comfort of loved ones, like the serenity of the deep blue ocean, be the oasis that forever surrounds our Bride and Groom. May they be well loved, and love well, letting the surety with which Water makes its journey to the sea, flowing over rocks or around trees, even turning into vapor and riding a cloud, ever serve as a reminder that with love all is well and will endure."

Malakai paused here to offer Tristan a chalice, which he drank from before placing it at my lips.

"Spirits of Earth, we ask that you give unto those you see standing before you this day, the rock-solid place to stand and fulfill their destiny. May their journey mirror the vast planes and fertile fields, expansive and alive. May they find the right seeds to sow to ensure

161

a bountiful harvest. And when they look up at the Northern Star, may they know that it is as bright and constant as their love for each other as well as the love of the divine is for them."

Flowers bloomed at our feet, spreading their joy throughout our small party.

"Father, Mother, Divine Spirit whose presence is felt in all things and at all times we ask your continued blessings upon this couple, upon their union and upon their family and friends who have gathered here to celebrate this joyous event with them. May they become one in truth and forever revel in the magic that is love."

Pulling a long ribbon from his pocket, he gestured for us to hold out our hands. Wrapping the ribbon first around Tristan's wrist, he repeated the gesture around mine.

"Remember that as your hands are fasted, these are not the ties that bind. The role already taken by the song your hearts share shall now be strengthened by the vows you take. All things of the material world eventually return to the Earth, unlike the bond and the connection your spirits share which is destined to ascend to the heavens. May you be forever as one in the passion and fire of you. Tristan, do you swear to uphold Reya's life and happiness above your own, for all time?"

"I do," Tristan spoke clearly, slipping an elegant ring with a single diamond winking in the golden light of the sunset on my finger.

"Reya, do you swear to uphold Tristan's life and happiness above your own, for all time?"

"I do," my voice was unwavering, sliding a matching band onto Tristan's hand.

'You are now as your hearts have always known you to be, husband and wife. You may kiss the bride!"

Applause and cheers rose up as Tristan lips met mine, our right hands still fasted together. When we broke apart, Malakai unwrapped the ribbon, placing it carefully on the small alter behind him, next to the chalice we'd drunk from.

"Ladies and gentlemen, it is my pleasure to announce; Mr. and Mrs. Tristan and Reya Amiri."

Tristan waited until the new round of applause died down before speaking again.

"It is tradition in our culture to hold a naming ceremony when there is new life," Tristan announced. "We have decided to perform that today, while our closest friends and family are here to witness."

Jared and Aden brought our children to the alter, handing them to Tristan and myself.

Malakai approached us again, a small bowl in his hands as he addressed our guests. "Each of you has written your well wishes for the children on bay leaves, which are renowned for protection and all around good fortune. It is tradition to write wishes on this herb before burning to make the wishes come true." Rubbing his thumb through the ash, he swiped it across our son's forehead.

"Named for Reya's father, I give you... Nicola Edmund."

He repeated the gesture with our daughter. "Named for Tristan's beloved sister, I give you... Leilani Rose."

There were wild cheers, then Jared, Aden and Jace knelt before us, bowing their heads. "We swear to protect you, see to your health and happiness, on our lives," they said simultaneously. It brought more tears to my eyes.

"Rise, brothers," Tristan acknowledged their commitment, clasping each in a hug.

Taking my turn, I whispered 'thank you,' in each of their ears before accepting congratulations from our other guests.

Ceremonies complete, a small team of caterers brought out food, and music swelled from large speakers that had been set up that morning.

We danced our first dance, and as he twirled me around the makeshift dancefloor, I looked into Tristan's eyes.

"I love you, Tristin Amiri."

"As I love you, Reya Amiri."

On the third song, Isy cut in to dance with me.

"You're doing really well with all the weirdness around here," I complimented her.

When Isabel and Ben had arrived, Tristan and I had decided to clue them in to a small part of what Elementals were. Since they'd already been privy to my special healing powers, it wasn't much of a leap for them to take in the manipulation of elements. We'd decided to leave out the shape shifting and longevity- there was only so much a person could take.

"That ceremony was seriously cool. When all those flowers popped out of the ground? Awesome."

"How's Matt doing with it?" I asked.

"It's a lot to take in, but it's difficult to ignore when you see it with your own eyes."

"I'm so glad you're here," I told her, hugging her tight. "Thank you for understanding."

After a few more songs, I excused myself to bring my children inside to feed. Tristan walked inside with me, our pace leisurely. I couldn't remember a time in all my life that I'd felt so content.

"Tristan," I glanced over at the love of my life. My mate. My husband. "I was thinking, for our honeymoon... I'd like to go to America."

"That's a lovely idea," he answered me. "I'm sure Jared, Aden and Jace would accompany us, as Jared was planning a trip to help Hugh anyway."

Smiling, I told him, "I think no matter where we go, we'll have at least Aden with us."

Tristan's brows grew closer together. "What do you mean?"

I let out a laugh at his perplexed expression. "You really haven't noticed how attached he is to our daughter?"

His head whipped between our daughter and the backyard, where Aden remained with the party. "You don't think..."

"Yes. I think the reason he felt so compelled to help me, felt so connected to me, was because of her."

"But... that's... she's our *baby*."

It amused me to no end that Tristan was having difficulty with this. "I would think you, of all people, would understand it better than me. You were already over 100 years old when I was born. What's the difference?"

"She's my daughter," he growled.

"And Aden doesn't look at her like that, yet. It's more like he's a super protective older brother. I'm not sure he's even realized the connection yet. Plus, in case you haven't noticed, she's just as attached to him."

Tristan continued to glare, but I knew he would get over it. The truth was, my human brain was a little grossed out over the idea that a grown man would be my daughter's mate. But, I wasn't human, and I couldn't put human limitations on my new life.

Tristan remained quiet while I fed our children, no doubt his head spinning with my revelation. No matter what, ultimately, it would be our daughter's decision, and I would make sure all parties involved understood that fact.

I also knew Tristan's anger would be fleeting. He saw Aden as a brother, especially after all we'd been through. It was Tristan's blood that changed Aden, and because of that there would always be a strong connection between the two.

Aden had recovered from the change after five days, and he seemed to be a natural at this life. Now that most of the operations that Donovan had been a part of had been shut down, I knew Aden was itching to find his sister. America seemed like as good a place to start as any.

As we were exiting the house, I caught sight of Jared, his face pale as a sheet.

"Jared?" I exclaimed, running over to him.

He was unseeing, his stare on a fixed point beyond me.

"Isy!" I called out, handing over Leilani to her while Tristan handed Nicola to Matt, before kneeling in front of Jared. "Jared? Can you hear me?"

Jace was at my side in an instant, but neither of us could knock Jared out of his trance. Laying him carefully on the grass, Jace began to examine him while I held his head in my hands, attempting to bring him out of it.

Finally, Jace looked at me and shrugged, finding nothing wrong. Pushing me aside, Jace brought his hand back and slapped Jared right across the face.

My jaw dropped open, but I quickly recovered when Jared began shaking his head as if to clear it.

"What is it, Jared?" I asked urgently. "What happened?"

"It's Hugh," his voice came out barely above a whisper. "He's gone."

"Gone?"

Jared began wheezing, racking sobs emanating from his chest. "He's gone, our connection is gone. I think... I think he's dead."

EPILOGUE

2 weeks later

Though the sun had set, the heat from the day remained. It was dry but not uncomfortable in the relief of night. As I stood in the middle of a desert, no civilization in sight, surrounded by Joshua trees and the sweet scent of creosote, I could sense something wrong.

Searching through the sparse landscape, I caught a glimpse of a shadow in my peripheral. Spinning, I searched for the figure that was just out of reach.

Whispers began then, fuzzy in their urgency.

"What is it?" I called out. "Who are you?"

Suddenly, there was silence, a woman appearing before me. Her haunted eyes were focused unerringly on me, her blood-streaked clothes in tatters.

"Help me," she mouthed.

Jolting awake, I reached out and grasped Tristan's arm, a gasp on my lips, tears streaking down my face. We were in a hotel room in Indiana, searching for clues on what had happened to Hugh. Our children lay sleeping beside us, undisturbed by my sudden outcry.

"What is it, *tau o te ate*? What has happened?"

"It's not what's happened, it's what's *going* to happen," I told him

His brow creased, Tristan asked, "You've had a prophetic dream?"

I nodded. "It's... it's your sister. She's alive. And she's going to need our help."

Dear Reader,

Thank you for reading *Immaculate: Book 2 of The Gifted Series*. I hope you enjoyed this second installment in The Gifted Series and join us in meeting the next mated pair, Reese and Dominic, in their book, *Night Shift*.

If you enjoyed this book, please visit Amazon to leave a review. It would only take a few moments and would help spread the word. A review would be greatly appreciated!

As always, you can keep up-to-date by "liking" me on Facebook, @anabannovels

Always, Ana

Other books by Ana Ban:

The Parker Grey Series

Abstraction; A Parker Grey Novel (Book 1)

Backfire; A Parker Grey Novel (Book 2)

Coercion; A Parker Grey Novel (Book 3) (available soon)

The Gifted Series

Allure of Home: Book 1 of The Gifted Series

Immaculate: Book 2 of The Gifted Series

Night Shift: Book 3 of The Gifted Series (available soon)

18462756R00105

Printed in Poland
by Amazon Fulfillment
Poland Sp. z o.o., Wrocław